Something emerged from the path behind Piper with a scream like a siren. It was gigantic, it was loud.

It was pink.

In that first instant, the only comparison Piper could think of was a megafauna equivalent of a flamingo, crossed with a fighting rooster. It had the long legs, the big beak, and the brilliant rosy plumage.

She tried not to giggle out loud at the image.

The critter was madder than hell.

# Demigod

## Blaze Ward

# ALSO BY BLAZE WARD

## The Jessica Keller Chronicles

*Auberon*
*Queen of the Pirates*
*Last of the Immortals*

## Javier Aritza Stories

*The Science Officer*
*The Mind Field*
*The Gilded Cage*

## Additional Alexandria Station Stories

*The Story Road*
*Greater Than The Gods Intended*
*The Librarian*
*Siren*

## Other Science Fiction Stories

*Mymirdons*
*Moonshot*
*Earthquake Gun*
*Moscow Gold*

## *The Collective* Universe

*Imposters*
*The Shipwrecked Mermaid*

## Collections

*Beyond the Mirror: Volume 1 Fantastic Worlds*
*Beyond the Mirror: Volume 2 Fantastic Worlds*
*Beyond the Mirror: Volume 3 Alternate Worlds*

# Demigod

## Blaze Ward

Knotted Road Press
www.KnottedRoadPress.com

For Shandy

# Author Note

When I made the jump from full-time fantasy to exploring science fiction, the first story I wrote was *Greater Than The Gods Intended*, starring a man named Doyle Iwakuma. That inspired *The Librarian*, which was the genesis of Suvi (Little Miss Librarian herself).

After that, we moved to Javier, Jessica, and Henri (plus Sergei Orlov, Hive, Tor, Eva, and Rick, but those are other stories).

I am happy to come back to this place, where it kind of all started for me. At the day job, there is a woman executive who concentrates on Diversity and Inclusion as one of her primary ways to give back to the generation coming up behind us. She was one of the people in the back of my mind when I was writing this story.

Let's face it, I'm a middle-aged, middle-class, dorky white guy. I have had a very lucky life, and been the unconscious beneficiary of that privilege. She's an incredibly tall black woman who's amazingly smart and won't take shit from anyone. She inspires me to be a better person, and I doubt she could pick me out of a police lineup.

The other driving inspiration was a conversation I saw online recently. The author was explaining to someone that the character was black. The fan drew them as a pretty, little, white elf girl. It got a little testy, because all the characters in the story were black (African-American, etc. I'm never sure what the LEAST offensive description will be with people I don't know, so please forgive my ignorance).

The two of them went back and forth for a considerable period of time before the author gave up in exasperation and the fan went on to do the whole cast as white people. And it wasn't out of spite, near as I could tell. The fan was just wrapped up in seeing the characters just like her. (Of course, she was a little princess to begin with, but hey…)

So that was also in the back of my head as I was writing. I had this fantastically-interesting (black) woman who deserved her own story, doing something that only she could do. That made it easy, being the only woman on the crew.

Because Piper was never just a supporting character to Doyle. She and Suvi would go on to be amazingly good friends over the decades of Piper's life. *Last of the Immortals* starts on Piper's birthday, I will remind you.

And I have challenged people to think about race and sexuality in a distant, science-fiction future. Humans are a species. Race is largely a geographic construct that quickly evaporates when you live in a big city and have friends that cover most of the spectrum (my gay friends fabulously cover ALL colors, I will have you know... <SNAP />).

So we need to think about where we are as a race. What pressures would cause us to roll back the clock and act like stone-age barbarians, living in fear and peeing ourselves whenever there is a strange noise. That is the opposite of science fiction, as I see it, but it is a "There but for the grace of God go I..." kind of approach to storytelling that needs to be explored more. We need to break out of our insular worlds and think about what it will mean when we are all born on a different planet, hundreds of light years away. Culture is still culture, but color is just chemistry.

But this is a story about growing up. It is Piper's story. I hope you will enjoy her journey.

bd
West of the Mountains
June 2016

# ONE

"Please tell me that this is all some sick, twisted joke, Doyle," Piper leaned forward and hissed, pointing one accusing finger at the man.

She would not grind her teeth. Not here. Not now. Not in front of these men.

Later, in her cabin. Maybe.

Maybe not.

Doyle stood rigidly still across the starship's chartroom table from her, face immobile, muscles standing out on his jaw. He was at least clenching his teeth, if not grinding them himself.

Anything to keep from yelling back at her.

Again.

The cabin was too tiny for the amount of anger it contained right now.

Piper was tall, taller than many men. Doyle was taller yet, a finger below two meters to her two fingers. Both of them were almost as tall as Piper's husband, even if they were both much lankier than her husband's solid bulk. But Bjorn was a giant.

Her skin was also lighter than Doyle's, a dark, rich brown. Chocolate, flavored with a kiss of caramel. Doyle's was bitter dark coffee with no hint of sugar or cream or softness. Bjorn's whiteness was so pale as to be almost pink in places that never tanned under the light of one of the many suns they visited.

Piper knew she looked like her grandmother Vanessa, Doyle's mother. Strangers on the street back home on *Zanzibar* had known her by those strong cheekbones, wide-set eyes, and pursed lips. She knew she reminded her uncle of the woman.

But everyone at the map table today was family: Piper, her husband Bjorn, her uncle Doyle, even cousin Stig, a Finn as pale as Bjorn, but another great-grandson of old *Papa Artur*, the grand fisherman who taught the whole clan to love space as much as he had loved the sea.

Still, she would not grind her teeth in anger.

"If you have a better idea, Piper," Doyle finally barked, "I would love to hear it."

Piper could see the exasperation on his face, in his eyes, in his hands. The latter looked like they wanted to reach out and strangle her.

Still, she couldn't help herself.

"Damn it, Doyle," she snarled at him, leaning forward to slam both of her palms flat against the metal tabletop. The whole cabin rang with the sound. "Have you seen how they dress here?"

Doyle leaned forward as well. "Do you want to be stranded on this planet forever, youngster?"

"No," she yelled back. "But you can't just order me around that way."

"I most certainly can, Piper," Doyle's tone was suddenly quiet.

Piper remembered when her uncle had grown quiet like that once before. Ten years ago, back home, when she'd only been thirteen, at a clan reunion outside *Ballard*'s capital city, Ithome, when someone decided to take umbrage that the daughter of the Ambassador from *Zanzibar* had chosen to marry a white barbarian Finn from the back end of beyond.

Alcohol-fueled words had been exchanged, growing slowly heated and loud.

And then Doyle had grown quiet. Pensive, even.

Right before he jumped the man and proceeded to beat his own second cousin bloody before several other men and women managed to pull him off the drunken loud-mouth.

"I am the Captain of this ship," Doyle continued in the most eerily-serene voice she could ever imagine fearing. "Your job title is Cook. That makes you the gunner and combat expert. And subject to my orders."

"But why me?"

Piper knew she should acquiesce. Felt it in her bones. But those bones were also *Iwakuma*, like Doyle's.

Stubborn, hard-headed bones.

At least Doyle's voice exploded again. That was probably safer, right now.

"Because I don't have anyone else that can do it, damn it," he yelled at her, a little spit-bubble flickering like a firefly and landing on the table between them.

"In case you hadn't noticed, there are no white people on this planet, young lady. Hell, even you're a little too pale compared to the natives."

Doyle hammered the surface of the table with an angry finger as he spoke.

"But the locals are a bunch of misandrist old hags who hate all men and nearly killed your uncle Jakaya the first time we came here. The only reason I'm alive today is because your mother's even crazier than you are."

That brought a ghost of a smile to her face, almost breaking the rigid iron masque. Doyle was not the first person to make that observation.

Which was saying something.

"No," Piper said, consciously willing herself to lean back, however much she wanted to reach across the table and throttle her uncle right now. "Why are we even on *Yaoundé*?"

Doyle leaned back as well and took a breath.

A fingerful of tension bled out of the room.

Hopefully.

"Stig?" Doyle prompted, almost back to mere command voice. Or at least in command of himself.

Close enough.

Piper turned as well, to look at her favorite crazy cousin, the skinny, dorky redhead with the booming laugh so out of place in that tiny chest.

"Something's gone funky with the nav computer," he said simply, the only tension evident showing in the whites of his knuckles around his bulb of hot tea.

"So restore from the backup," Piper said harshly. "That's what it's for."

"I don't know when it went started," Stig admitted, turning a shade of bright red that Piper could never hope to emulate.

She felt the weight of something ugly settle around her shoulders. Like a three-days-dead herring, heavy and stinky.

"And?" she hesitated, finally. There was no beef with Stig. He was just a genius doing his job as Ship's Carpenter. There were no better engineers on their homeworld of *Ballard*.

"And we can either continue to blunder around the *Spinward Reaches* until we find what looks like the path home," Doyle interjected. "Or we come here and get our hands on a known-clean copy."

"They're just going to give it to us?" Piper's voice started back up the ramp to loud.

"No," Doyle said simply, quietly. "You're going to go steal it from them."

"No, damn it," Piper snarled. "I am not. I tell you what--"

Bjorn's hand coming to rest on the back of hers shocked Piper sideways.

Her husband did not often choose to interrupt family and crew squabbles. For all his size, he really was more of a gentle giant. A quiet, non-technical farm-boy from the inland suburbs who had gone into space with her. Because of her. For her.

Piper lost her voice, turning to look over at him in shock.

He had a presence like a blond Buddha, piercing green-gray eyes conveying a wealth of warmth and emotion that always seemed to somehow cut through her rages without leaving any marks.

"I think," he began quietly, barely above a whisper. "Perhaps it would be best if everyone took a break for a while. After all, we're safely hidden here where the natives won't find us, and we're not going anywhere."

She watched Bjorn turn that same calm serenity on Doyle.

"And it's Stig's turn to cook dinner," the blond giant smiled, turning her silently without ever losing contact with Piper's hand as he guided her towards the hatch.

Piper decided to let her teeth start to grind.

If her husband thought he was going to talk her around to Doyle's point of view…

# TWO

Piper really wanted a door that she could slam shut as she followed Bjorn into their cabin. The efficient little pneumatic bulkhead door shutting quietly on well-maintained rails lacked the raw, thumping sound of her anger, echoing through the ship.

Bjorn turned left and went past the bathroom door and into the main chamber, easing off his slippers and crawling immediately up onto the oversized bunk in what Doyle had christened *The Honeymoon Suite*.

Piper did not feel remotely honeymoonish.

"What are you doing?" she snapped at him.

"After watching you and Doyle argue for thirty minutes," he replied calmly, "I'm tired. I don't know how you two do it, but I need a nap."

Piper started to snarl something, and stopped herself.

Had they really been at it for thirty minutes?

Automatically, she checked the clock readout on the wall.

At least thirty.

*Damn it, Doyle. Why me?*

Bjorn slid his butt back against the inner bulkhead and patted the mattress invitingly.

"Do you really think I can sleep right now?" she snarled, only semi-sarcastically.

"No, *mrembo*," he replied. "You are too wound up, too angry, too stubborn. But I want to cuddle up around someone warm and soft so I can sleep."

Piper took a breath to continue the argument, and caught herself.

Bjorn was helping, in his own calm way. Water to her fire. Stone channeling her lava.

She blew out a breath and stepped close to the bunk.

Bjorn silently held out a hand to her. She took it, warm, calm. She could feel a tear's worth of her own mad rage begin to subside.

Piper nodded and took another breath.

Yes. A nap would be helpful. Dinner was going to be another raging altercation with Doyle and his stupid ideas.

She crawled up and slid her rump back against Bjorn, letting his arms enfold her. At least he kept his usual groping to a minimum. For now. Instead, his warmth cocooned her.

"So why are you so angry, beautiful?" Bjorn said sometime later, waking her up from a doze.

Wait, sleep? Really? How could she have fallen asleep at a time like this?

"Have you seen how they dress here?" she said. The fire was mostly gone, but the embers were still underneath, like reefs just below the water at low tide.

"I've seen you wear less at the beach, woman," her husband teased quietly. "That's not it."

No. It wasn't, was it?

That was just the native attire of a warm planet with a planetary civilization just barely above Bronze Age. Those were a dime a dozen in this sector of space, blessed with terraformed worlds that had sustained humanity *After The Fall.*

Doyle and his crew weren't this far out for First Contact and trade. That would come later.

They were out here trying to be the first to locate ancient caches of technology that could be used to bootstrap *Ballard* and *Zanzibar*, her two homeworlds, back into the Galactic Age, having just barely crawled within reach of Interstellar only two generations ago.

They were out here trying to get rich.

Piper shivered. Bjorn tugged her close enough that he was breathing in her ear.

"You can tell me, you know," he whispered. "I'm not legally allowed to testify against my own wife."

That got a chuckle out of her. Not everything done by the crew of this ship, *Ngoma Mwisho, The Last Waltz*, was probably entirely legal, according to the old codes of interstellar law from the days of *The Concord.* But what happened out beyond the deep frontier was usually rough and dangerous.

And occasionally very profitable.

Piper took a deep breath and probed her own self deeply.

Why was she angry? Why the bitter words and rage with Doyle?

But she already knew the truth. Had known it all morning.

She rolled inside Bjorn's arms, ending up face to face. He had apparently eaten a peppermint drop at some point today.

She could let him see things in her eyes, her face, that the rest did not. His soft hands promised the cool solidity of freshly-turned earth on her back.

"I don't know if I can do this, Bjorn," she whispered, pressing her face against his broad chest and pulling her hands in on herself.

There. The fear. The vulnerability. How did this man bring that out in her? How did he know?

"Right," Bjorn rumbled. "Because you're such a bumbling little ditz who can barely tie her own shoes."

"What?"

"Let me tell you a story, wife," he continued.

She was close enough to feel the laughs in his belly that never made it to his mouth.

"So, there I was, sitting in this bar one night, drinking beer with some friends and watching the game," he began. "This pretty girl walks in. Two of them, as a matter of fact."

"A girl?"

"Hush, you," he said. "All the best stories start with pretty girls in bars. So there I am, maybe a sheet and a half to the wind. It was a really good night."

"Uh huh. You?" Piper grinned lightly into his chest.

"When I was younger, you understand, and much dumber. So anyway, I started hitting on this pretty girl, in my own magical, drunken way, but she wasn't having any of it. She was brusque and aloof. And me and my friends got carried away. You know, catcalls, propositions. It got rude and out of hand quickly."

"And then what happened?" Piper asked, making her eyes wide with implied innocence.

"The usual thing that happens when a group of drunk guys get mouthy with a pretty girl in a bar," he replied. "She walked right over to our table and got up in my face about it, which is saying something, because she turned out to be one of the tallest girls I've ever met. And then we got stupid."

"Did you now?"

"Stupider, maybe. Anyway, this pretty girl and her almost-as-pretty cousin proceeded to beat up me and my three best mates, right there in the bar. Knocked one guy out cold. Threw another one over the bar. Left me on my back on a carpet of peanut shells. And you know what I said to her, looking up as she was sitting on my chest, getting ready to punch me again?"

"*Marry me*," Piper said. "Which is still the dumbest thing I've ever heard."

"It worked. You did."

Piper just shook her head. It had. She had. Possibly the smartest thing she had ever done.

Who would have imagined?

"So why are you telling me this, Bjorn?"

"Because my dangerous badass of a wife apparently doesn't think she's tough enough to walk into a barbarian town and steal something from a bunch of hicks."

"Violence is never the solution, Bjorn," Piper said.

"I'm sorry, *mrembo*, but violence is frequently the solution," he retorted. "Probably not the best solution, or Doyle would seriously consider hovering over the entrance to one of the tunnels with plasma thrusters until we cooked everybody in the place dead and could just walk in and take what we needed. That's always an option for some people. But not Doyle. That's why I will fly with him."

"So you think I can do this?"

"I know you can do this," he said. "Hells, I expect you to make it look embarrassingly easy."

Piper felt his kiss on her forehead.

Yes. That was why she had married this man. So he could talk her into breaking into a temple and stealing a god.

# Three

Doyle looked up warily as Piper and Bjorn came into the ship's aft saloon, overlooking the tail of the ancient, little, converted *Concord* minesweeper. Normally, they ate in the compact galley, large enough for the four of them, but Stig had convinced him to make this a special night, so Doyle had gotten out the good service, right down to the long, linen tablecloth Stig insisted on having ironed.

"Chili?" Bjorn sniffed hesitantly.

"You're the one who decided to make him cook tonight," Doyle responded with an evil smile.

Genius engineer Stig might be, he was still a lousy chef. Anything more sophisticated than tossing ingredients and spices into a pot to stew for several hours was a risky roll of the dice. And even something that simple might be pushing it.

Doyle was rewarded by a wary nod of Bjorn's head in acknowledgement that some plans don't always work out so well.

At least Piper looked calm.

Doyle had spent several hours in the chartroom that afternoon, trying to find a way home. Unlike the rest of the salvager community, he still believed in keeping paper star charts printed in an old notebook.

The problem was that the original information was more than two thousand years out of date and hadn't been that accurate to begin with. They were in an area that had barely even been charted back when civilization still existed, and *Yaoundé* wasn't on any of them.

Suvi had promised to print him better charts, one of these days. He just hadn't gotten around to taking her up on it. Now, he had to get home so they could figure out what had gone wrong.

If Piper failed, he had one, last, long-shot he could play. Borderline-stupid, but probably good enough. It still might be years getting back to *Ballard*, if they ever did.

Best to save that news until necessary.

Doyle nodded to his niece and sat her and her husband facing each other on the sides of the long table. The saloon had walls painted a soft, creamy tan, and a nice, blue carpet designed to formally entertain potential investors and local big-shots. The table would hold twelve comfortably, and could be extended to seat another eight, since they were on the surface of a habitable planet and could safely prop open the double hatch to the Observation Deck.

Overkill, but tonight needed to be one of those evenings where everything was formal and polite.

The energy had gotten a little out of hand earlier. That girl was definitely an Iwakuma.

Doyle cracked open a bottle of wine and poured, bringing Piper's eyebrows up, even if she did remain uncharacteristically quiet.

"This voyage has been hard on everyone," Doyle said to the room, loud enough for Stig to hear, but looking right at Piper. "I thought we should have a night as a family. Good friends, good food, good memories."

Bjorn raised his glass to echo the toast. Piper joined him. Doyle raised his.

Stig staggered in with a pot of fresh chili and thumped it onto the table.

"Let's chow, people."

α

Piper took a deep breath and set her spoon down. Stig had managed a passable pork chili tonight, which was an accomplishment for him.

She raised her wine glass in a halfway-mocking toast of Doyle, seated across the table next to Bjorn.

"I would really like to hate you right now, Doyle," she began with a sly, sarcastic tone. "Especially since you're right. My mother warned me about you being right."

That got a chuckle out of everyone. Ajali Iwakuma-Laakkonen, the oldest child, had gone out into deep space with Doyle and their brother Jakaya, searching for the loot of the galaxy. Today, she was the Managing

Partner of Iwakuma Salvage Interstellar, back on *Ithome*, making sure they all stayed on the beam.

Piper had heard mom's stories, growing up, between the long trips. Uncle Thorson, the chandlery attorney, had told Piper more of them. Jakaya had even started writing wild science fiction thrillers about the family's exploits, but mother had assured her that much of it was grounded in experience. Some of it was even toned down to make it believable fiction, but still accurate.

Especially the parts about Doyle being right.

"If *Yaoundé* has turned into such a bad place, would it be better to destroy it?"

She couldn't help the edge of challenge in her voice. That was the one option she hadn't satisfied herself on. It wasn't like she hadn't killed dangerous barbarians on other worlds. Most recently, *Kel-Sdala*, where they had rescued an immortal pixie *Sentience* from a bunch of shoot-first lunatics armed with poisoned arrows.

Doyle got a serious look on his face. His skin almost turned the color of coal as he flushed.

"Not my place to decide that," he answered. "The climate here makes it a hard place to survive. People get hard in response. Very thin margin of survival. If they didn't have something we absolutely needed, I'd be happy to have never come back here in the first place."

"And yet, here we are," Piper said.

There was no apportioning of blame. Just an observation that they were in a place, and only she could get them out. And not her usual way: the liberal application of violence and firepower.

She would have to use guile and diplomacy instead.

She could do this.

Growing up sucked. Although, at twenty-four years standard, most of her land-locked friends were already starting families. *White-picket-fencing*, she called it.

Maybe it was time to start acting like an adult.

Piper eyed Doyle as she spoke. This ship might be a family affair, and had been long before any of the rest of the current crew came along, but Doyle was still the Captain.

A fair captain, but a hard man.

"I'll do it," she said simply. "But I want some time to prepare. And I'll need all of your help."

She felt like she was stepping off a cliff, asking for help from anyone else, but she had come to realize, wrapped up in Bjorn's warmth, that she didn't always have to be bullet-proof. It was a feeling as frightening as it was liberating.

"With?" Bjorn asked.

She hadn't told him anything. His job was Boatswain. He handled all the little day-to-day tasks on the ship, maintenance and cleaning and inventory.

One of the strangest parts of committing salvage in a dark and fallen galaxy, at least when the two of them had first joined the old crew, was the costume closet.

Not every planet they visited had managed to keep a human population. Those that did had rarely made it as far back up the technology scale as the Iron Age. Only *Saxon* and *Pohang* had managed to reboot themselves as far as Industrial. In another generation or three, one of them might have found *Zanzibar* first, instead of the other way around.

Most planets were Stone Age, or possibly Bronze. And usually insular, violent, and xenophobic. Like *Yaoundé*.

In addition to all the other things she loved about him, Bjorn was a pretty good seamstress.

"Break out the bolts of cloth, big boy," she laughed at him. "We're costuming."

He nodded at her. Their fate was pretty much in her hands at this point, which added a little bit of intoxication to the flavor.

"Doyle," she turned to him next. "These women are heavy god-ridden, right? Primitive, sky-worshipping types who believe in magic and tell stories of the lost colony they escaped from?"

Her uncle shrugged.

"*Fled from* would be a better term," he replied. "But yeah. All the usual sociological trappings of a small cult in a harsh land, beset by hostile forces. It's pretty average, that way, other than total matriarchal domination."

"Good," Piper smiled, turning to the last person at the table. "Stig, I want you to make me look like a warrior hero, like the old Greeks did it."

He was twenty, dorky, and smart. She watched Stig's blue eyes grow devious, with that little half-grin he got when he was up to no good. Which was most of the time.

"What did you have in mind, Pip?" the redheaded engineer asked slyly.

"Suvi showed me how to rebuild a pulse rifle with a stun setting," Piper said. "I want you to amp the craziness up another notch."

"Oh?"

"The height of technology around here, and the most common weapon, looking at the records, is a spear," she said. "I want you to make me one, but I want you to bury a pulse rifle in the shaft so I can point it at someone and strike them down with a lightning bolt. And a stun setting."

Piper considered a planet like *Yaoundé* as she worked up a head of steam.

"And it's freaking hot around here, and nobody wears hardly anything. I've seen the bimbo pictures you draw, Stig. I want you and Bjorn to make me something like a chain mail bikini, but I want a cooling system built in, top and bottom."

"Bikini won't work," Bjorn leaned forward suddenly and rested his elbows on the table to think. "If you want armor, it should be a bandeau, maybe with pauldrons attached over the top, or that traditional thing where a woman wraps a single loop of cloth around her neck, and then both breasts. Can't remember what they call it, but that would be better, especially if we need to put in a radiator fin somewhere for bleeding heat. Same for a bikini bottom. You'll actually want more cloth, not less, and a big belt."

Bjorn's eyes also got a far-away look as his voice trailed off. He and Stig put their heads together and started jabbering away in an arcane tongue of cloth and bias and drape and wiring.

"You're good with this?" Doyle asked quietly as the other two men got lost in their conversation.

Piper could see the concern in his face, normally a rigid casting of dark bronze that revealed nothing.

"I am," she said, as much to convince herself as to her uncle, her captain. "It's the only way."

She smiled and took a breath. Being a grown-up might suck, but being responsible felt good.

"But when we get back," she continued. "We're definitely talking to Suvi and a few other people about how to come off to barbarians like this as badass sorcerers or something. I'd rather be a freaking goddess, next time we have to do this."

"Technology advanced enough is indistinguishable from magic," Doyle retorted. "Maybe that's what the ancient gods had, you know."

# Four

From the outside, the ship looked like a giant, steel-gray, hammerhead shark, even down to the two eyestalks sideways off the bridge. The original ship had been a *Concord* minesweeper, designed to fire a great, big gun backwards at mines that could frequently shoot back. The sensor rigs needed that level of parallax for accuracy. The ranges for playing that kind of game safely were stupid.

Today, Piper was happy to be resting in the shade of the great, vertical tail, between the engines and under the maw of that giant cannon's bore, the Mauler.

It was hot on this planet. Not murderously so, but easily 45 degrees out in the sun and something close to ninety percent humidity, most of the time. It was only in the false dawn that the temperature outside ever got lower than Doyle normally kept it inside.

Piper was out again today, getting acclimated to it. The only way to do that was to exercise outside. Stretching. Katas. Yoga. Jogging in the mid-day heat.

And trying not to look as foolish as she felt.

Stig and Bjorn had outdone themselves, this time, a masterpiece of cloth and leather.

But she still felt stupid wearing it.

They had started with lace-up sandals that looked primitive, but molded to her feet, and had a lightweight, armored, cooling element built in and insulation underneath. According to Stig, she could stand on a stove for twenty or thirty seconds without feeling it or damaging her feet.

On her shins, Piper had two woodchucks. That was the only way to describe them. Working from old pictures Doyle had saved, and ancient references, they had made her fur leggings that ran from knee to ankle, and appeared to be made out of the pelt of some bushy, furry critter that had been golden-brown in life. Underneath, they had shaped armor plates like greaves, and added another cooling system as well.

But it still looked like she had a pair of woodchucks humping her legs.

True to his word, Bjorn had made her a matching leather bandeau and boy-shorts loincloth, both in a maroon color that accentuated her naturally-creamy dark brown skin. Trust her husband to fabricate her an outfit guaranteed to make her look sexy as a barbarian.

Both top and bottom had a tough, ballistic cloth sewn on the inside, capable of stopping small arms or turning a knife, and a cooling system with radiator fins that would keep her skin cool for several hours, once she powered them up.

Around her waist, a belt rode low. Hanging from it was what Piper could only call the bottom half of a cloak. When she was standing still, it hung all the way around her to mid-shin, leaving only the front of both thighs open to wind. In the swamps below, it would protect her legs and butt from things that might scratch.

And look good. Weird, but good.

The top of the bandeau was below Piper's collarbone, so Bjorn had added a complicated shoulder harness in hardened leather, and then extended it down her right arm for greater protection. It looked like dragon scales, a set of six progressively-smaller, riveted panels down to her right elbow.

On both wrists, the boys had created bracers for her. They looked like polished bronze, because they had been electroplated with it, but the stuff underneath was hull-grade steel, protecting a variety of interesting electronics not limited to: a radio, a short range sensor, and a small cutting laser designed to kill locks and small critters too stupid to run away.

Piper normally wore her hair almost shaved on the sides, and perhaps two centimeters of curl tall on top. She should have cut it three weeks ago, when they first landed on this planet, but things had gotten too busy, and then she realized she needed to change her look to go with her new outfit.

With a little work each morning and a pick, she had a passable mohawk, seven centimeters tall and growing more menacing every day. She considered dyeing it, but had left it black for now.

On her forehead was the best part. It looked like a large, smoothly polished stone, nearly four centimeters across, perhaps an onyx except it was too blue, resting in a gold setting. Four thin, gold chains held it in place, two just above her ears and two around her mohawk. Inside was a small sensor pack with a camera and a transmitter, so the boys back here could see and hear what she did.

Piper thought she just might keep it after they left, it was so cool.

Goddess, indeed.

Now if she could just convince herself she was capable of taking on an entire planet of man-hating barbarian women, all by herself.

Today, however, she was feeling awfully close.

Piper had adapted one of her normal weapon kata routines to use a spear: thrusting, stabbing, slashing, blocking, and pummeling. The weapon wasn't wood, but instead a rough-surfaced carbon-fiber shaft painted up the right color, with a big bronze cap at the bottom to balance the sixty centimeter double-edged, hullsteel, leaf blade at the top.

A local tree had been stumped off, and became her target dummy. It felt good to take out all of her aggression on it. This stupid planet. The bitter old hags who would sacrifice an un-bonded male rather than trade with him. The nasty, hot jungle waiting for her in the swamps below.

*Ngoma Mwisho* was hidden in a high vale on a relatively dry and wind-swept plateau. They had water, sunlight, and a few wild fruit trees close by, but nothing larger than a tree shrew, according to all the paranoid sensors on a very subtle salvage vessel.

The big stuff lived below. Down below that green carpet that extended to every horizon when she walked over to a nearby ledge to look down. Getting down would require time and possibly a rope. Nobody would come up here without a reason.

And the crazy ladies on this planet didn't have a reason.

Not yet.

*Maybe after I tweak their noses. Then they'll loosen up a little and... And what?*

Piper couldn't imagine those people relaxing and turning this land into a paradise on Earth. That would require them to be friendly and polite to foreign travelers.

After the way they had treated Doyle and Jakaya, Piper didn't see that happening without a serious revolution.

And she didn't have that kind of time or energy.

Tomorrow, she had to go talk or sneak her way into their greatest temple, and desecrate their holiest relic with her greedy, foreign cooties.

There were moments when she thought about bringing in the big guns, about just killing them all.

Then she wouldn't have to dress like this in public.

# Five

Isioma considered the spoor before her as she kneeled in the middle of the path, her bow strung and nocked, just in case.

There were two sets of tracks in the loamy soil.

The newer mark was obvious. A Devilbird. One of the big ones, too, from the span of the toes. Perhaps eight feet tall and weighing in at something above two hundred pounds. One of the grand, dangerous matriarchs of the deep jungle. A vicious, pink, killing machine, with a beak that could shear bone, eighteen centimeter dewclaws on both heels, and toes like clawed hands when the monster balanced up on one foot to grab its doomed prey.

It was the older set of tracks that drew her eye. They were human prints. Some female had passed this way earlier. Isioma's own moccasins would leave a mark like that, but when she put her foot in one of the prints to compare, the tips of her toes barely came to the base of the other woman's big toe.

How huge must that woman be, to leave a print like that? Six feet tall? Seven?

*Truly, Onye buru ibu. She who is a giant.*

From the sign on the jungle floor, the woman had passed an hour ago, traveling at a slow pace. Someone unused to navigating the green depths. She had left broken stems and twisted bladegrass in her wake.

Obviously, a stranger to the swamps.

*And in profound danger.*

Isioma wondered if the woman knew she was being stalked.

The Devilbird had her scent. Isioma could see the occasional marks of a bone-shearing beak in the sandy soil, pressed down to confirm a scent mark.

Meat. Prey. Domination. A woman of victory, like all of *Nri.*

Under her breath, Isioma snarled.

*Nri.* Home.

There was no sanctuary on this world but *Nri,* her people, her tribe, safe within *Ugwu,* the Mountain That Protects.

If she could manage, Isioma would never set foot in *Nri* again. Find a man she could take into the sunlight, escape the reach and wrath of her sisters, those long tentacles of deception and slowly-strangling death, and find themselves a place beyond the great swamp. There was a whole world out there, beyond the mountain facing the deep swamp.

Isioma had lived in the swamp long enough to know that those who had once stalked them, unseen in a hundred generations, had never gotten this far. But no females except her and a few others ever made it out of sight of the mountain.

Maybe they had given up. Maybe had fallen victim to their own evil.

It was safe to live aboveground. Not that anyone believed her.

Or rather, at least as safe as the feather-grass sea ever got, with Devilbirds, Flared Snakes, and the great reptiles that hid in still waters.

A rumble sounded in her ear, causing her to glance back over her shoulder.

Felix transfixed her with those baleful, green-eyes stare, as if asking why they were sitting here when there was a Devilbird to track. The great lion shook her tremendous golden mane and rumbled again.

Isioma stood and reached way up to scratch the mighty lion, her own little personal kittie-cat, right in that spot atop the skull, between the ears. More purrs.

Onaedo, the Goddess Avatar, might have taken her mother away from her, but Isioma was still a daughter of the blood. Felix was bonded to her, would protect her, would have eaten her cousin when Onaedo ousted Adaobi as leader of *Nri* and Goddess Avatar.

Isioma shuddered.

Had she been an Initiate in those days, already bound to the Order and living in the Temple itself, she might have been killed as well. But a lowly Supplicant, even one of the blood, slept outside the Temple complex.

She had fled into the night, into the swamp. Gotten away before they could make her disappear permanently, like her mother had.

Since then, she had spent as much time away from *Nri* as she could, out beyond the hidden gardens and camouflaged rice paddies and grain fields.

Out in the swamp.

In five years, she had grown into a woman, just as Felix had grown from the size of a house cat she had been that night to the mighty warrior she was now. More importantly, they were both hunters, valued by the traders in *Nri* for the meat Isioma brought back, the hides and feathers and trophies.

The Devilbird was not her prey. No one in their right mind went after the Devilbirds, even with a familiar that had been *engineered,* to use the ancient holy word, from a wild, dangerous beast, into a house cat, even if Felix was ten times the size of those in the Temple, or all of *Nri*. The great cat's eyes were five feet off the ground and looked down on Isioma.

Still, the Devilbird was stalking a woman. It behooved her, them, to aid this female, this creature, this giant from legend, if for no other reason than to see her in person.

Nobody Isioma had ever met had feet this big.

# Six

Piper swore quietly.

The path down the mountain had been a king-royal bitch. Rappel down a steep face without breaking her neck. Drift crossways over a zone of gravel just aching to turn an ankle or break a leg. Then finally hike down into the hard, green jungle below, those ugly steam baths at the base of the mountain that just wanted to sauté her.

It had taken most of a day to get to the edge of the swamp and find a place to sleep, protected by a couple of ultrasonic screamers supposedly good enough to drive away all creatures, with motion detectors and ultra-powerful strobes built-in to wake the dead.

At least she had managed to catch a little sleep. A couple of hours, pretty shallow. It was too hot, too yucky. A week like this and she'd probably vote to clear the place with pulse rifles; social stability and Doyle's non-interference practices be damned.

Now it was mid-morning.

She hadn't seen the sun yet today. Only enough light that filtered through the dense canopy, forty meters overhead, to light up some sort of packed-dirt game trail that was headed in the right general direction.

She took a moment to calm herself.

*Another day, just like the rest. You can do this.*

The swamp was on her left as she walked with care, with stand after stand of trees on her right as she crossed other game trails, clearings, and little creeks and wadis. She had her spear pointed forward, pulse rifle setting. So far, she had left the safety on.

So far.

There were strange creatures in the darkness of the trees around her. Panicked, angry, or mating. Hopefully, they were just angry birds and chipmunks, and nothing bigger.

Something wheezed.

Behind her.

*Trouble.*

It sounded like Stig's tea kettle boiling. That low whistle building and climbing into the range of painful.

Piper couldn't imagine anything that made a sound like that in nature.

Piper found herself in the middle of a sort of clearing. Maybe a beach. Twenty-odd meters long, bounded by water on one side, thick with mangrovy kinds of trees, and maybe eight meters wide. It was filled with low grass, the kind of open space shaped roughly like those fat, green beans that Bjorn liked to grow in the hydroponics lab. As good as any other place.

Piper two-fisted the spear and found the pulse rifle trigger with her left hand and flipped the safety off as she watched the trail behind her.

Something emerged from the path behind her with a scream like a siren. It was gigantic, it was loud.

It was pink.

In that first instant, the only comparison Piper could think of was a megafauna equivalent of a flamingo, crossed with a fighting rooster. It had the long legs, the big beak, and the brilliant rosy plumage.

She tried not to giggle out loud at the image.

The critter was madder than hell.

She knew that on some worlds, the original terraforming packages had gone weird. Too much radiation, not enough balance in predator/prey relationships, something off.

So, giant, pink, carnivorous, flamingo-ostrich. With long, freaking spikes on the backs of its ankles, and claws wider than her foot was long.

It had stubby wings that it was using for balance, but they would never lift the thing off the ground. The bird's crest was at perhaps two and half meters high, putting those big eyes in the tiny head roughly at the level of her forehead.

For a moment, the creature just stared at her, as if unsure she was actually prey. Maybe it had never seen a human before.

Many solitary, Earth-descended predators were all about size in their psychology. If you puffed up and made noise, it might frighten them, make them retire.

"Go away!" Piper yelled, jumping and waving the spear at it.

That apparently wasn't the right response. Pink monster thing reared its head back and screamed to the heavens.

She hoped that someone was monitoring the audio channel in her forehead gem.

The monster started to charge, toes digging up turf like a giant, pink chicken scratching for bugs in Grandpa Laak's front yard.

Piper had no interest whatsoever in finding out what it would be like to get close to this thing.

She fired her first shot, and watched it blow up a tree twenty meters away.

*Crap.*

And then the beast was upon her, with a beak like an axe lashing out.

All those years of kung fu, aikido, and ballet that Piper had complained about as a child paid off right now.

She threw herself to one side and somersaulted across the damp ground, rotating around the spear like an axle and popping right back up, ready to fight again. Just like her mother had always told her would happen, once it became automatic.

So now her mother was as right about things as her uncle. This was just not her day.

Fortunately, a critter that big couldn't turn on a dime and get to her before she was up again.

Instead, it crashed into a small tree, knocking it over, the moist, soil and root ball thrust up into the air, before the giant pink chicken could spin again.

Piper flashed out with the tip of her short pike, poking the damned thing in the drumstick, thinking winter turkey thoughts.

That pissed it off even more.

*What do giant doom peacocks sound like normally?*

*Okay, maybe that was a cry of pain.*

*Whatever.*

Her ears were ringing, and everybody in a kilometer knew they were here. Or maybe that the big bird was having a successful mating ritual.

You never knew on strange worlds what things might sound like.

The bird turned and took a bite at her hands.

Piper pulled the spear back fast and let the beak close on the leaf blade instead.

They played tug-of-war for a moment, before Piper got shifted around to her right and *pushed.*

Nobody likes a paper cut on the tongue. Not even giant, pink chickens.

It let go of the blade and goggled at her, like nobody had ever held it to a draw before.

*Tough luck, princess.*

Maybe it had eaten everyone else it had ever encountered, and hadn't ever run into anything big enough to scare it.

Still, it screamed instead of biting again, flaring its wings out and trying to look bad-ass. Maybe trying to scare her off instead.

*Seriously, Flamingo of Death? My sister hits harder.*

Piper stepped back and triggered another shot with the pulse rifle.

This time, she hit the damned thing.

And knocked it on its ass.

*Shit. Stun setting. Must have pushed the wrong button.*

Piper took a quick moment to look down and find the fire selector switch on the lance. She flipped it back to pulse rifle setting and aimed her spear for the killing shot.

An arrow out of nowhere slammed into the peacock of doom and nailed one wing to the bird's body. A second one, a moment later, pierced a lung with a splash of brilliant crimson.

The bird gave her a piteous look and let go a soft, mournful cry as a third arrow struck it in the heart.

Piper spun to her right as the big, pink, doom chicken died and pointed her spear back up the trail.

A girl stood there, proud and fierce but tiny, a native with an old-fashioned composite bow and a fourth arrow in her hand, with a quiver on her hip.

The stranger's skin was even darker than Doyle's, almost true black in tone, but otherwise, she wore an outfit similar to Piper's.

Bright green leather bandeau over small breasts. Pauldron-looking leather piece over both shoulders, in a darker green, hooked in front with two really cute, big, brass buttons. Loincloth-looking thing around the waist in a light green. Wide leather belt with a quiver, a short blade scabbard, and several pouches. Brown, leather, knee-high moccasins laced up.

There were only so many ways a girl could do fashion in this heat.

That fourth arrow was nocked, but the girl hadn't drawn for a shot.

Good thing. That would get her the same thing the flamingo got.

Piper looked close and realized that she was facing a woman, not a girl. She had hips and muscles that no child developed until she grew up. Even Piper had gotten hips, eventually, after all her lanky height came in.

The stranger was maybe a meter and a half tall, barely up to Piper's shoulder. And maybe fifty kilos soaking wet.

And she had a look that landed somewhere between confusion, awe, and anger. Piper remembered her mother occasionally giving her that look, although usually heavier on confusion and anger at an obstinate teenage daughter.

*Iwakuma.*

A moment of silence stretched.

The woman spoke.

"Onye na chi aha ka i bu?"

Piper let her confusion show, cocking her head to one side, even as she kept her spear dead-centered on the tiny woman.

The stranger showed her own confusion.

"Who in Goddess name are you?" the little woman asked her slowly in stilted Spanish.

Who, indeed.

Piper had found the natives.

# Seven

Isioma stopped herself from drawing the arrow she had already nocked. The giant had already struck down the Devilbird with a magical bolt from her spear. The tip of that fearsome weapon was pointed at her now.

Instead she nodded politely.

One did not challenge giants and demigods without good reason.

The demigod nodded back and appeared to relax.

A little.

"Nzinga," the giant woman replied in the slaver tongue, the language of hated Sanmarco. "Thank you for your assistance in slaying the great flamingo. What is your name?"

Isioma considered, and relaxed as well. The female giant did not look like the ancient slavers were depicted. She was not white.

"I am Isioma, daughter of Adaobi," she said carefully, unsure what the demigod would do next.

It was a good answer. The giant seemed to relax.

A moment later, the demigod's energy returned.

"Get down," she called sharply. "Lion behind you."

Isioma was shocked. The demigod spoke the forbidden tongue now, the Temple Language.

And her spear was coming up to cast another lightning bolt.

"No," Isioma yelled, dropping her bow and waving her hands in the air. Isioma moved quickly sideways with the tip of the spear.

The demigod seemed to be trying to protect her.

"She is mine," Isioma continued, frightened at what the two powerful beings might do to each other.

Isioma turned her back on the demigod and faced Felix, poised to charge into battle for her, to protect her.

Lions did not understand demigods.

"Down, Felix," she commanded fiercely, waving both hands towards the ground to get the cat's attention. "Now."

Felix rumbled harshly. Isioma feared the cat would provoke the demigod, unknowing of the terrible vengeance the giant might unleash.

"I said down, Felix," she repeated, letting her mother's voice ring through her frame and echo off the trees.

Felix heard it as well, felt it, knew it

The great lion stopped in place and squatted. Her feet weren't underneath her, but at least she was willing to listen. With a few angry rumbles.

She was a cat, after all.

Isioma walked close and reached out to scratch Felix between the ears.

"Good girl," she said.

Felix's eyes half-closed as her rumbles slowly turned to purrs.

"That thing's with you?" the demigod asked in a voice of quiet wonder.

Isioma pivoted so she could keep scratching, and still talk to the giant stranger.

"I am of the blood," she replied simply.

Even a demigod would know what that meant.

"Are there others like that?" the woman asked carefully.

Isioma glanced back at the hand pointing at Felix.

Others? Oh.

"No," Isioma replied. "Only daughters of the blood will be so bonded. My mother had one when she was a child. I do. Perhaps my daughters will as well."

"Wow."

The demigod had come a few steps closer.

Enough that Isioma could see the woman's face clearly.

It shocked her.

The demigod's flesh was unscarred and unpainted.

She had a headpiece, but the chains seemed sufficient only to hold the gem to her forehead. It was not attached to the bridge of her nose, like Isioma's was.

Isioma suppressed her shock and allowed only the curiosity to evidence itself.

Her own face only bore three scars: each cheek and the center of her forehead, all three less than half an inch long, as had been appropriate for a lowly Supplicant to the Order, once upon a time. Initiates and Beloved bore many more scars.

As an adult, Isioma had subsequently limited herself to only a septum piercing with a single, silver ring, and the bar through the bridge of her nose connected to the fine silver-chain headpiece around her skull, above the ears.

Like those of *Nri* who were not of the Order, she had painted her nut-brown face with white stripes, a ring of radiating, two inch, white lines around the base of each cheekbone, plus the center of her bottom lip and four dots down her chin.

This creature, this giant, this demigod's face was naked before her.

The shock was almost too much to believe.

Isioma considered her history. The slavers of Sanmarco had been light skinned. *White.* They had been dominated by unbonded men. And they had not been known in the sixty generations since *Nri* had fled to *Ugwa* to hide.

*Thus we have survived.*

"Nzinga," Isioma tasted the name, speaking the Temple language carefully. It had been years. "I am Isioma. This is Felix."

Felix rumbled her own greeting. Isioma could see one paw slowly shifting under the great body as she began to relax.

"What did you do to the Devilbird?" Isioma hesitated, pointing at the pink corpse.

This was dangerously close to provoking the demigod, but her curiosity won out.

A moment passed.

The demigod, Nzinga, did not seem angry, nor confused. Perhaps her question had only barely verged onto the province of the gods?

"In another moment, I would have slain it," Nzinga replied carefully. "It was too stupid to know fear."

"The Devilbird admits no rival," Isioma said carefully.

She seemed on safe enough ground, for now.

But what would provoke this stranger? This demigod?

What did she want?

# Eight

Piper considered the tiny woman and the great, big cat.

*Big cat?*

None of Doyle's stories had covered anything like this, beyond the tininess of the natives.

Seriously, the woman might be one-hundred-fifty centimeters tall. Hell, the cat was taller. And friendly. Friendly?

Pussy-cat the size of a giant lion. Friendly?

Still, she was here. She had met one of the locals. This was the opportunity to go for guile and subtly instead of firepower. Prove she could do this thing.

*Easy, right?*

At least they spoke Kiswahili locally. Or a flavor close enough. Plus Spanish. And something else Piper had never encountered. That was probably pretty normal. In the *Days Before*, those two had been part of the seven major trade languages in the galaxy, but every planet had its own tongues. And the old homeworld had known hundreds more.

Still, Piper was obviously not from around here, and needed to communicate to the native girl.

*Diplomacy. Be like Doyle. Even if it kills you to admit he's right.*

"I come from a far distant land," Piper began, getting into the whole thing about playing a bad-ass sorceress named Nzinga.

It was an ancient, cultural name she had pulled from the history files on the ship when she was setting this gig up. These people were supposed to be insular, but might have legends about an ancient queen, a woman so named.

Every little thing helped.

The native woman, Isioma, got twitchy. Even the cat picked it up, got perfectly still.

Piper made sure her hand was on the pulse rifle trigger. If this whole *I come in peace* thing didn't work, kill the cat first, deal with the girl next.

"Sanmarco?" Isioma asked.

Piper watched Isioma's fingers twitch, ever so slightly, but the hands didn't move. Any wrong movement right now might be lethal. For someone.

Sanmarco? San Marco? Planet, city, or person?

The girl spoke Spanish, so probably a place name instead of a person. Doyle had said nowhere else on the planet was inhabited save the strange city burrowed into the mountain like a termite mound. All the natives were descendants of folks who had fled someplace, probably this *Sanmarco*, before the fall of mankind.

Talk about old hatreds.

*You are a sorceress, girl. Act like it.*

Piper decided to go for broke.

"No. I was born on *Zanzibar*," she replied carefully, watching both of them over there for any reaction. Any movement that might provoke the pulse rifle.

None.

She watched the girl mouth the syllables silently to herself.

Good. Totally unknown, as opposed to a likely enemy requiring action on the girl's part.

Something had sent this culture down the path it had followed, where it hated all men and all outsiders.

Something named Sanmarco. Or someone.

*Now, how to make the girl an ally?*

Doyle had called it a Temple. That old ship hidden inside the warren of tunnels. They had managed to trip an identification beacon as they landed. It had identified the presence of a ship, but nothing more. One that identified itself as *The Temple*.

And nothing more.

And even that signal would have been well hidden to anything but the sensors on an old minesweeper keyed up to *paranoid*.

*Calm. Cool. Steady. Like you know what you're doing.*

"I need your help," Piper continued.

If this girl, this woman, was friendly, it just might work.

If they were all crazy here, better to find out now, when Piper could blast them both and hopefully get away, instead of when she was trapped inside the hillside with all of them.

"You speak the Temple language, the language of the *Beloved*," Isioma replied. "It is forbidden to any but the Order."

Order? Forbidden? Kiswahili? Talk about backwards.

*And you speak something I've never heard, and couldn't pick up fast enough to pass for a native, even if I was as small as you.*

*Whatever.*

*Bad-ass sorceress from the stars. Go for broke.*

"It is the language of the heavens, Isioma, daughter of Adaobi," she said. "Of the stars, and the darkness between them. There are other languages, other worlds, but this tongue is one we speak on *Zanzibar*. If you speak it, your kin might have come from somewhere like it originally, as well."

Or, somewhere close enough. We're all children of the homeworld.

Piper let the girl process that while she studied the cat, watched that tail swish forcefully, nervously.

The feeling was mutual, a vague antipathy held in check until violence became necessary. Maybe she too was just a kittie-cat, at heart.

Bjorn would probably agree.

"What aid to you seek?" the girl asked.

Piper presumed, from the slow way she spoke, that the native woman was not used to Kiswahili, and had to assemble things in her native language and translate them before speaking. Kinda like how Piper would feel going into Spanish.

Nobody spoke Spanish in this sector of space, as far as they had found. Even *Before*. Where did these people originate?

*And now, let's roll the dice.*

Piper made sure the spear was centered on that damned cat. Or rather, where it would be if it suddenly sprang forward to charge her.

She'd played that game before.

"Do you know what a computer is?" Piper asked carefully, using the oldest version of the word available.

She was rewarded by the girl's eyes getting HUGE.

Isioma made a sudden gesture that nearly got her shot, dropping the bow and placing the backs of both hands flat against her forehead, fingertips touching.

*Must be a religious thing.*

"The voice of the Goddess," Isioma whispered.

*Voice of the Goddess? Seriously? Whatever.*

"It is only a machine," Piper continued. "I must speak with yours."

Isioma grew even more frightened, sitting perfectly still and shivering as she listened.

Sure enough. Bronze Age barbarians, wallowing in the ruins of their own civilization.

Lost in corrupted memories, instead of rebuilding the machines and tools to get back to the stars.

*Lazy gits.*

But at the same time, Piper watched the girls eyes quickly grow shrouded and she turned her head down and to the right. It was a sneaky look. Mean.

If Isioma had been looking at her like that, Piper might have just blasted them both and taken her chances with the next local she met, but that tight, evil smile on the girl's face was directed at someone else.

Someone with whom that girl had some serious bad blood going on.

Piper smelled an opening she could hammer a wedge into.

"Is it forbidden to speak with your Goddess?" Piper asked, a shot in the dark, based on nothing so much as the girl's behavior.

Isioma flinched at the words.

*Bingo.*

"None but the Goddess Avatar, and the senior-most of the Beloved, the Adepts, may speak with her," Isioma said forcefully, her voice turning angry. "All others are forbidden."

The way the girl bit off the words said a lot. Anger. Bitterness.

Bad blood.

"Perhaps that should change?" Piper continued.

More shots in the dark, but this girl had never played poker for money. She was almost an open book.

*I feel like Doyle.*

"The Order controls *Nri*," the girl said. "Ugwu, the Mountain That Protects."

Pre-Darkness colony? Twenty-five hundred years of solid isolation? Maybe more?

"And those you still hide from?" Piper prodded slowly but relentlessly. It was almost like dealing with one of her pre-teen nieces. "Have they ever found you?"

"No," Isioma said tightly, angrily. "Never."

"I will share a secret with you, Isioma," Piper said, reveling in her role as sorceress.

She gestured grandly at the sky, with the hand not touching the pulse rifle trigger.

"Out there, among the stars," she said. "There was a grand war between the mightiest gods, fought a thousand of years ago. Many worlds were utterly destroyed."

Piper fixed the girl and her cat with a steely gaze.

*Subtlety and guile.*

"I was surprised that humans still walked on this world, this place you call *Nri*, when so many other places were simply annihilated. I have never even heard of a place called Sanmarco in my travels."

Those eyes got HUGE again, this time with an audible gasp that caused the cat to flinch in empathy, rather than anger.

*Seriously. Taking candy from babies. And kittens.*

And yet, the girl had a big cat, and a bow, and had done a nice job killing that stupid, oversized, pink chicken.

Grown woman. Young, but grown up. Dangerous, even.

Just never exposed to the docks on *Ballard* or *Zanzibar*. Never really been anywhere tougher than this swamp.

*Your loss.*

# NINE

Isioma could barely contain herself.

*Destroyed? Worlds?*

The Goddess Avatars had mentioned none of this. Neither her mother, Adaobi, the former queen, nor the woman who replaced her, the current Goddess Avatar, Onaedo, had said anything about a war among the gods. Let alone one great enough to annihilate whole worlds.

Had Sanmarco survived?

For a moment, Isioma let her imagination unlock those secret dreams of finding a man, breaking him free of his place-bondage, and living a life above ground, sharing him with no other woman.

And yet...

Was the demigod a demon sent here to tempt her? To lead her astray?

There had been others.

Isioma had heard the tales.

Strangers. Strange men. Giants.

Unbonded.

*Giants...*

Was Nzinga of them?

Were there other demigods out there, tempting the children of the lost into apostasy?

Could she trust this extraordinary titan?

She was a stranger, after all. An outlander.

Isioma was tall for her kind, standing nearly an inch above five feet. Only Onaedo was taller, that she knew of. And even then, only barely.

Nzinga was over six feet tall. She would walk the corridors of the ancient Temple and find them to her size, the land of giants. The ancient tables and chairs, the metal kind that did not require footstools, would be comfortable to her height.

*Were we all such a height, in ages past?*

*Has* Nri *fallen so far, hiding from the sun, from the stars, from Sanmarco?*

*Were we all demigods, once?*

Isioma gestured carefully at the stranger. She could see the tension of imminent violence in Nzinga's stance, so like the Devilbird in that way.

"You speak dangerous words, Nzinga," Isioma said carefully, trying to keep the many emotions out of her voice.

She could envision a thousand possible paths: liberation, vengeance, freedom, betrayal.

And she had only the word of a strange, giant woman upon which to judge.

And Felix, carefully seated next to her, providing warmth, but resting on a fulcrum to spring if necessary.

Isioma watched the tip of that deadly spear.

She could see what Felix did not. Her cat's first movement would be into death, not rescue.

So. The demigod could know fear. Fear of Felix.

In a way, that made her more dangerous.

It made her human.

The gods were said to be abstract, distant, aloof beings, unconcerned with the affairs of everyday women.

Only humans connived so diligently.

And Nzinga lacked the scars of initiation, or the paint of her majority.

Isioma kept seeing her as the child she herself had been until she could paint the rays of the sun on her cheeks and chin.

This demigod was a dangerous, dangerous creature.

The Devilbird paled by comparison.

"Why must you speak to the Goddess?" Isioma continued as this demigod waited.

"I would ask her why she had not told her daughters of the fall of the galaxy," Nzinga replied sternly.

Truly, a battle of wills between the Goddess and a demigod awaited.

Would Nzinga bring down *Nri*?

Would that make her life better?

"Only a Beloved Sister, an Adept, may speak with the Goddess or her Avatar," Isioma said. "You and I are not even Initiates."

Isioma nearly quailed under that stern gaze.

"Your Goddess has told you lies," the demigod accused. "Or her Avatar."

*Mother!*

Isioma nearly snarled out loud before she contained herself.

*No. Adaobi had been bound to the Order, of the Order. Their secrets, their confidences, had never been betrayed, even to her only daughter, Isioma.*

"How will I know you speak the truth?" Isioma asked, ready to judge this stranger on a tilted scale and possibly throw her life away to prevent a demon from accessing the Holy Temple.

And yet...

This demigod might free them from Onaedo's grip.

Isioma could envision herself prying answers from that woman, Avatar or not, about a night five years ago when Adaobi disappeared, and a new Avatar was crowned in her place. A night a barely-woman-child named Isioma had fled into the darkness and hidden in the swamp for days that turned into weeks before she dared return to *Nri*.

Hers was a pleasant vision, blood dripping slowly from painful cuts in Onaedo's arms and legs as Isioma plied her with questions.

The demigod smiled serenely.

"The Goddess will speak truths to you when I ask," she said calmly. "If we cannot simply walk in and ask the sisters of the Order, are there ways that you and I could ask the Goddess alone?"

Isioma gasped.

How could any but a demigod know about the hidden chamber?

Her mother had sworn her to secrecy.

"Can you not even trust your Goddess to speak truths?" Nzinga pressed.

Her words were like the blows of a hammer on Isioma's mind. A great bell ringing and ringing inside Isioma's skull.

Petty, childish dreams of vengeance suddenly seemed within reach.

She could guide this stranger, this giant, this demigod, to *Nri*, take her to the heart of the Temple itself by little-known, hidden ways she had barely visited in years.

She could have answers.

And if the female was a demon, sent to lead them astray?

Where better to betray her, than deep in the bowels of *Ugwu*, the Mountain That Protects?

# TEN

Piper held her breath and waited.

She could see emotions play out across Isioma's face, surge and recede in her eyes.

Seriously, this girl needed lessons in how to play poker if she was going to be a grown-up.

Still, on balance, positive.

*Okay, maybe I can do this.*

*Stranger things have happened.*

The girl had some serious personal issues that needed addressing. And it looked like she was happy to use Piper as a hammer to get those answers, presumably from the woman in charge.

*Not like Doyle hadn't ever had me play bad cop.*

Fearful, God-addled barbarians. Hiding in the warrens they had carved out millennia ago, afraid somebody named Sanmarco would find them.

Where men were kept place-bonded, whatever that meant.

Gnarly, ugly kind of world.

Isioma reached some consensus with the voices in her head.

"I will take you to the Goddess," the native girl announced, firmly but quietly. "We will seek the truth."

Piper figured she could relax a bit. The girl put her hands on the cat's spine and levered herself upright.

"Felix," Isioma said, leaning close and speaking loudly, sternly to the big, yellow hairball. "The demigod is a friend. You will heed me."

*Demigod? Awesome. Wait until I tell my captain and my husband that I'm a demigod, now. I hope they're listening to all this.*

The cat rumbled.

She watched Isioma pick up her bow and carry it left handed as she approached the dead doom-pigeon.

"We will need to take time to collect trophies," Isioma announced. "May I?"

*May you what? Strip the damned thing? Oh. Trophies. Right. Go for it.*

Piper nodded. This kill apparently belonged to the demigod, even if Isioma's arrows had done the trick. Being able to catch lightning bolts would be kinda impressive.

She watched the tiny woman draw a shortblade from her hip and expertly slice. Wings came loose. Feet. Those damned dewclaws. Skull.

Piper was amazed that the other woman was able to remove all of the chest skin, with feathers still attached, in a single piece. That was some serious carving skill. This girl knew her taxidermy.

"You are a stranger to *Nri*?" Isioma hesitated.

"I come from a world where a single, vast ocean covers almost everything," Nzinga replied grandly.

"I have never eaten the meat of a Devilbird," Isioma announced. "There is too much to carry home, but it would be criminal not to take some."

Fresh, homemade, chicken fingers. Maybe forty kilos worth from one ugly bird. Damn, that would be one hell of a party.

"I agree," Nzinga replied. "Does Felix eat offal?"

Isioma glanced up guiltily. She nodded tightly.

Seriously? What do they feed great, big, kittie-cats, if not giant, dead, pink canaries?

"She should dine like a queen, then. No?" Nzinga decreed her own grace on the situation.

It was only a few more minutes to finish stripping the parts they wanted, and then Piper watched Isioma approach the water of the swamp carefully and wash her hands, eyes alert for gators and other things.

Felix took a long moment to understand that she was allowed to have what was left of the 'bird. Then she jumped in with all four paws.

The crunching sounded like a small forest being run over by an angry tractor. A big, furry tractor, happy as a pig in fresh mud on a hot day.

Kittie.

"Are you an agent of chaos?" Isioma murmured suddenly as they watched the cat gorge herself.

"I am an agent of change, Isioma," Nzinga replied. "All systems require some chaos, lest they degenerate into stasis."

That sounded like something Doyle would say, anyway. He was full of useless banter about big ideas.

*Too many books.*

Isioma nodded, apparently lost in deep thoughts of her own.

The cat finished her lunch.

She rose silently and paced her way towards them, licking her lips happily.

Piper found her hand on the spear again, caressing the button of the trigger in a very private manner.

Damn, that lion was big.

She got closer and stopped, staring at Piper and purring as it squatted on its butt.

Purring?

Not growling. Not rumbling.

Purring.

Weird.

It seemed to want a scritch.

*Oh, what the hell.*

Piper let go of the spear with her off hand and dug her nails into the fur at the top of the skull, where she had seen Isioma work.

Sure enough, those purrs got LOUD.

"She accepts you," Isioma announced with a nervous titter.

Both women let go breaths at the same time, and then laughed at each other's mutual discomfort.

Something broke inside them both.

"Come," Isioma said suddenly, finally warm. "Let us go talk to a Goddess."

# Eleven

Termites.

Seriously. A whole freaking mountain filled with giant termites.

Piper suppressed the giggle that almost erupted out of her mouth. The native girl might take that the wrong way.

*You're a demigod. Act like one.*

*Whatever that is.*

Ugwu, the Mountain That Protects. Wasn't that what the girl had called it?

In her head, Piper flipped the local topography around to match up to the reality in front of her.

Another day and then some walking to get to this point.

Egg-shaped valley. Roughly.

The whole basin kinda looked like an impact crater from low orbit. Slam a bolide a couple miles across into the planet at a pretty flat angle and you'd get a pucker like this after a couple million years of erosion.

Enough rain and it turns the shallow bowl into a swamp. Just like this.

Ugwu was at the narrow end, a big ugly lump of stone sticking out like a thumb from the lesser mountains on either side of the neck. Great, big swamp behind the two girls, a slowly-draining basin bleeding water away to the east, eventually emptying into a small, inland sea a couple hundred kilometers away.

The morning sun would catch the place as it cleared the horizon and light it all up.

*Probably looked like a weird skull when the sun was just right in the summer.*

Piper could also see where someone had brought down a good chunk of mountainside at some point.

"The Temple," she said, addressing herself to Isioma, crouched between Piper and that cat on the reverse slope of a nearby hill, watching the mountain age. "It brought you here from Sanmarco, once upon a time?"

"That is the legend," Isioma replied tightly.

Piper could hear the rough emotions under her voice. Bad time to be having a crisis of faith.

Or, maybe a good time.

Revolutions were rarely ignited by happy, contented women.

*Behave yourself.*

"And the tunnels of the ancient Temple are metal, while the rest of the complex is stone, right?"

"Correct."

"So. My assumption is that the ship is probably about forty meters wide from your descriptions," Piper said, thinking more out loud than expecting an answer from a Bronze-Age chick. "Maybe three hundred, three-twenty long. Five or six decks?"

"Meters?" Isioma's face was scrunched sideways in confusion.

*Crap. What do they use here?*

She touched her hip and thigh to indicate her leg, and then her waist.

"This is about a meter long," she said. "I'm just under two meters tall."

That set off a strange and complicated discussion about scales, lengths, measurements, and everything else that took ten minutes to wrap itself back into meters.

*Seriously. Barbarians.*

But she was closer to right than wrong, considering the girl's memories were years out of date and she had been shorter then.

So.

Large-sized freighter, since the description included only two grand cathedrals originally, with one transformed later into living space and a school using local wood instead of metals.

That sounded like twin cargo bays hanging either side off of a central spine. Original powerplant and engineering at the deep end under the mountain, backed into the parking place they had blasted into the mountain side. Bridge and computer core close to the front.

The Goddess.

It made sense. A cruise ship would have been all small spaces. This sounded more like a slave revolt that had turned into a mutiny, especially from some of the legends Isioma had told her as they hiked closer.

Run away and end up here. Burrow deep to hide from the slavers.

*There were some evil shits loose in the universe, in the old days.*

*And it hadn't gotten much better since.*

The founders had brought down an avalanche to cover the original tunnel, then shored it up and dug a new, smaller entrance and dozens of access tunnels and rabbit holes every which way, with whatever tools they had been able to build or improvise, before slowly collapsing back to barbarism.

And they had survived for at least twenty-five centuries down here, so they were doing something right. They had to be tough little shits themselves.

At least the two women and the cat had found a good place to wrap up that huge hunk of bird, along with the other trophies, and bury it. It should be safe enough there, at least until they could come back for it.

Piper felt the need for a barbarian princess headdress made out of pink feathers.

Just the sort of thing you wore to High Tea, back home in Ithome.

"So how do we get in?" Piper finally asked, grinning at the girl.

This had gotten beyond demigod and rogue warrior babe. They had accidentally turned into something closer to sorority sisters planning a beer run while being under-age.

Not that Piper had any experience with any such outrages against the law.

*Not at all, officer. All on the up-and-up.*

"You do not wish to speak to any of the Beloved, nor the Goddess Avatar?" Isioma asked with a hint of longing.

*Yup, that programming went deep. And no, I barely trust you and me. Let's leave the others out of this.*

"Would you trust them to speak truth?" Piper asked carefully.

Having the girl a little riled up was one thing. Angry enough to chew nails was probably pushing it.

*Probably. Maybe not.*

Isioma fixed her with a look that said a lot about what this native girl's mother had probably looked like, before.

Hard. Cold. Tough.

Maybe her own mother, come to think of it. Certainly Grandmother Vanessa.

"Yesterday," Isioma retorted. "I probably would have barely trusted them. Now, I would seek my wisdom from the Goddess herself."

*At the tip of a knife* went unsaid, but Piper could see it in those eyes.

*Ya know, subtlety and guile work pretty well when someone else gets to be the heavy. Maybe that was why Doyle always took me out to visit the natives.*

*Crap. That means he was right then, too.*

Piper harrumphed in her head.

"Okay, so what's the plan?" Piper continued.

Their conversations had been weird already, a day and a half spent crossing the swamp, sleeping with the big kittie and the night sensors. Cook some of that bird to munch on for breakfast. Talk a bit. Stop. Keep walking. Pick things up again twenty minutes later as if nothing had happened.

At least the girl was getting better at her Kiswahili.

"We shall circle in from the left," Isioma replied, lost in thought. "There are rice fields and fish ponds we need to skirt, so that nobody gets a good look at you up close. The Mountain has several old access ports high up, in areas not in use any more."

Piper chalked that up to the slow decline of the culture. They had a whole planet to take over, and still intended to stay hidden in their little termite mound, come hell or high water.

She wondered if the planetary terraforming was failing, too. Three thousand kilometers north of here, it would be lovely. The equator was probably unlivably hot. At least by humans.

Maybe gators were making a slow comeback. They had on some worlds.

Isioma rose, grabbed her bow, and scratched Felix on the head.

Piper did the same, amazed at how well she had fallen into the rhythms of this place, these people.

Not people. Ants.

Yeah, ants.

A whole nest of females, outnumbering males three or four to one. Females doing all the work in the sun and the fields, while the men were kept in special barracks until they were old enough, and then kept inside at safe and quiet jobs except when they were farmed out for occasional stud duties.

Piper was sure men back home would think it to be a lovely life, servicing your own harem.

*Must be boring as shit to have nothing to do but stay in shape, read, and only rarely get to go play.*

Still, not her planet; not her problems. Probably.

*Bad-ass sorceress demigod from the stars might have something to say about the value of the whole socio-political edifice.*

*Something* Unpleasant.

# TWELVE

*What will it be like to hear the voice of the Goddess again?*

Isioma quailed a little, inside.

It was one thing to speak of forcing answers to troubling questions from recalcitrant lips.

It was something entirely else to be the one holding the knife.

But there needed to be answers. Many of them.

Words about Goddess-wars, galactic dark ages, isolation. Explanations as to why *Nri* must of needs hide on an empty world from seekers no longer cognizant.

Isioma rose and reassured Felix. Her companion was at least as intelligent as a child, if lacking the subtleties of advanced planning. A particularly bright seven-year-old, if you will. Dangerous, but well-meaning.

Nzinga followed behind, letting Isioma set the pace and direction.

She had timed their walk today to arrive on the side-slopes of Ugwu late in the afternoon. The sun was just about to pass behind the mountain's shoulder, running into the long twilights of spring.

There would be light enough to move, but dimness thick enough to mask the demigod from prying eyes below.

Once in the caves, any contact would be troublesome. They could neither of them hide their presence in the forbidden tunnels.

Best they did not have to. Thieves in the night.

She had been called that, more than once, by Onaedo and others.

Tonight, it would be a truth, rather than idle rumor and insinuation.

Still, she had a demigod by her side. One who could slay, or choose not to kill, as she determined. One who might be the liberation of this world.

What might it be like to live beyond *Nri*? To see other lands, other worlds. To live with three other males as Nzinga apparently did? To be bonded to only one, but to not share him with any other females?

To be free?

The Goddess Avatar, and the Goddess herself, had much to answer for.

α

The stone was sure underfoot. Isioma had worried that unseen, entropic weathering on the slope might have caused issues.

The ancients had used their magical lightning bolts to carve the tunnels, rather than mattock and shovel. It left behind passageways straight as plumb lines, but occasionally had them emerge from the brow of the mountain in strange places, on unsafe slopes.

Isioma paused as they approached the mouth of the beast.

Well below them, at the base of the slope, the river emerged from its underground dwelling and slowly poured over the rocks into calm pools, before emptying into the greater depths of the green swamp. No square lines had been added to the ground, lest they stand out when overflown by enemy eyes. Nothing to give them away.

Instead, fish ponds had been dug or adapted, and then blocked off with wicker weirs that mimicked beaver dams. Rice paddies had been planted and flooded, but left in an almost feral, shapeless state.

Again, hiding from prying eyes. Eyes that might never come.

Isioma wondered again what *Nri* might be like if they could expand their efforts at agriculture and pisciculture, without fear. Just grow so much protein that everyone could eat as much as they wanted without having to weigh their society against the total calories they could produce.

What would it be like if they could afford to have as many man-children as they wanted, instead of a carefully proscribed ratio?

If they could be free?

The Goddess had much to answer for. And her Avatar.

She shrugged mentally and turned to look into the tunnel before her.

It was tall and skinny and squared off, as if a narrow door had once closed it off. The proportions reminded her of the demigod.

Nzinga was built thus.

Isioma passed through it and studied the space within. As with all of *Nri*, the lights of the ancients still glowed, high on the walls. Unlike the tunnels farther down the mountain's face, these were spaced well apart. Pools of illumination only occasionally interrupting the darkness rather than a tunnel of light.

"Interesting," Nzinga's voice called her to stillness.

Isioma turned to see the demigod studying the edges of the opening.

Felix sniffed casually, her own curiosity drawn, but unable to grasp whatever had distracted the giant woman.

Isioma waited while Nzinga ran hands carefully over the sill and then dabbed at the walls with the tip of her spear.

After a moment of soft digging, a small avalanche of dirt fell, causing Felix to spring backwards in an awkward surprise that nearly gave Isioma a giggling fit. The lion's sneeze was even funnier.

"There it is," Nzinga seemed proud of herself.

"There what is?" Isioma asked as she approached to see.

Inside the sudden hole was a worm. Or something.

It was half the thickness of her smallest finger, and ended in a splayed-out fray like petals of a tiny gray flower.

"This was wired for a hatch once," the demigod pronounced.

Isioma understood that she had forgotten so much of the Temple language. Each of those words was understandable. The phrase was meaningless.

Nzinga glanced over and saw her confusion.

"There was a door here, once," she continued. "It was controlled from within the Temple itself, connected by this wire all the way down to the Bridge."

*The Inner Sanctum once reached this far?*

*And someone had removed it? And done what?*

Isioma cursed bitterly inside, where the demigod hopefully could not hear.

*We tore it out for the metal, because we could not make more from the materials of this world.*

*Thus, we have fallen from the heavenwalkers.*

"So they cannot sense our arrival?" Isioma hoped aloud.

"That would be my guess," Nzinga replied.

The demigod pointed at the rough, packed-dirt floor.

"There are no tracks here," the giant continued. "And the sconces are spaced for maintenance and not functionality."

Again, the words lacked coherence. But the demigod seemed pleased. That seemed to indicate that their task might become easier.

"Felix," Isioma nodded, turning to her companion. "Stalk."

The great cat's nostrils flared. Slowly, she moved deeper into the tunnel.

Isioma watched a small breeze blow the lion's mane back softly, emerging from the depths of the darkness.

One of the reasons she had chosen this entrance was the benefit of a chimney effect. It was the highest entry into Ugwu. Heat from the Temple would rise and escape, providing her companion with the scents of the interior as they moved inward.

It was akin to stalking the Devilbird. And probably as dangerous.

But she had a demigod at her side.

And if that failed, a knife.

# Thirteen

The call to evening prayers brought Onaedo up from the inner peace of her meditations.

She rose languidly, letting each joint unfold from her lotus. That was the secret of her youthful looks. Daily meditation in the lotus position to keep the mind firm. Regular exercises in the privacy of her chambers for her skin and muscles.

She stopped and drank heavily from a glass of wine an Initiate had left earlier. A quick moment to fortify herself before heading down to engage with the harpies who coveted her throne.

*Nri* was a wild beast, always looking to turn on its rider and devour her. As she had once, before she became Goddess Avatar.

Those who had originally aided her own rise to power so many years ago were not always happy to only come up one stair. The landing just below power was no more satisfying for them than it had been for her.

Fortunately, the Goddess had helped her to eliminate those sisters who would not wait their turn, and to neutralize the rest.

Ugwu could only protect so many souls at once, after all. If there would be more children born, then the elderly must give way.

Onaedo smiled.

Not everyone wanted to give way.

But the Goddess Avatar would not be thwarted.

She checked her appearance in a wall-mounted mirror.

Four decades rested lightly on her dark brown brow, with her curly, black hair only barely starting to develop a fringe of white rings underneath.

Similarly, her face still had just enough plumpness in it, despite the long, dark leanness of the rest of her body, to make her wrinkles shallow and soft. And the hundred scars across her brow and cheeks just accentuated the warm depths of her brown eyes, and inviting smile on her lips.

When she chose warmth.

Even bearing a girl-child had only hindered her looks, her body, a little, and then only enough to inspire her to spend the last few years returning to the peak of fitness with the same iron discipline she brought to all tasks.

A woman to be respected, as well as feared.

But always feared.

Onaedo adjusted the fall of her dark blue linen tabard over her black leggings and considered leaving her legs bare for now. Her chambers were always pleasantly cool, but the air could not stir as well during evening prayers. The cathedral would grow warm and stale after the first hour, and require the empty depths of the night before it cooled back down, just in time for morning prayers.

And she displayed the supple strength of her legs if they were free.

Yes, tonight she would show off, just a little. Enough to remind the others that she was still dominant.

Onaedo stripped her leggings off, leaving only her black loincloth and a strip of black cloth tied around her breasts underneath the fabric of the tabard. Her skin was still tight over hard muscles, unlike some of those harpies who had let their power and jealousy overcome their natural discipline.

Those would be the easiest to cow, but the most dangerous, as they could see their own shortcomings writ in her flesh.

Onaedo smiled cruelly.

*Fools.*

She put on her Goddess Avatar face and stepped to the ancient, white, metal door to her chamber.

It opened with the faintest swish, allowing her into the hallway that ran just behind the cathedral.

It was one of the few of the ancient doors that still worked on its own, and the first one always repaired, even if other doors had to be sacrificed in the process.

Anything for the Goddess Avatar.

# Fourteen

Piper let the stillness of the dim tunnel embrace her.

Felix, Isioma's lion, had a musty smell to her fur. Dust and sand and wilderness.

The very slight breeze from deeper below brought the scent to her nose as she followed Isioma down the faint slope, into the heart of Ugwu.

The other woman had her own distinct fragrance. Sweat on the skin and oils in the hair, on a world where strange critters might lurk in the water, ready to jump out and eat you, so you couldn't just jump in for a quick shower or bath whenever the mood struck you.

Piper figured she would smell the same way after a few more days without a shower.

The thought of living without showers summed up the rank uncivilized nature of this place.

*More than electrical lighting, hot baths would be the first thing I invent.*

She smiled to herself.

*Barbarians.*

Isioma had asked her not to slay anyone they met by chance in the tunnels, so the pulse rifle was on the stun setting.

Unspoken was the assumption that they might not just tie up anyone they met, after Piper took them down.

At least it wouldn't be her to blame for extreme violence, as much as she thought it might solve the problem. Maybe Bjorn was right.

*Crap. They were* all *right, weren't they?*

Ahead, the cat came to a stop suddenly and crouched down, rumbling almost inaudibly. Isioma moved up on one side and squatted with hand on the lion's spine, so Piper took the other.

The cat was warm beside her as she touched it. Must be cool in here.

The three of them waited in the dimness for several moments.

Piper couldn't hear anything, but after two days in the swamp, she knew enough to let the two hunters, the two experts, handle things. After all, she expected that same courtesy from Doyle when they were in the field together.

"There are three others ahead of us," Isioma finally whispered, leaning across the cat's back. "A Beloved sister and two Initiates."

*Three? How in hell can she tell that?*

Piper nodded sagely, just in case.

Apparently, the tiny woman really was an expert on this sort of thing.

Piper relaxed and waited.

"They have passed and crossed into the other tunnels now," Isioma whispered, rising.

Piper and Felix rose as well.

"Shortly," Isioma continued. "We will enter into the ancient Temple itself. The stone floors will give way to metal and the risk of discovery will go up immensely."

Isioma paused for a moment, scowling, before she continued.

"All should have gone to evening prayers now. The halls ahead should be clear."

Assuming nobody was late to the party and blundered into the three of them in their rush.

Still, those were the risks and rewards for breaking into a temple. Even if the place sounded more like a prison than anything.

Piper reached out her off hand to touch the wall in the dimness between lights. It was an ancient stone, almost a granite from the feel.

Sometime in the distant past, the tunnels had been created with energy-faced excavation tools. The surface had that queasy feel, almost wet under the fingertips, but still dry. Polished first by heat, and then age, and finally personal friction from the occasional passing shoulder. But still undeniably stone.

Different. Barbaric. When they got into the ship that brought the original settlers, it would be like coming home.

Her own ship was very similar. Well, Doyle's ship, but *Ngoma Mwisho* was a family enterprise, and she and Bjorn each owned their own shares.

Their exploration vessel, their home, had started life as a *Concord* Minesweeper, sometime over two thousand years ago, serving in that navy for generations before being decommissioned and left on *Icaria*, along with six of her sisters, in what had been a breaker yard at that very moment when galactic civilization was destroyed, and with it, most of humanity as well.

Doyle and two of his older siblings had managed to strip parts from the other six corpses to make the best one fly again, so that they could head out deeper into the wilds and find more treasure.

The vessel that had brought everyone to *Yaoundé*, the Temple, had been a rough contemporary of *Ngoma Mwisho*, possibly even built in one of the yards on old *Ballard*, Piper's other home, back when it had a thriving ship-building industry that concentrated on space, rather than water, as it had for the last several centuries before space flight returned.

How many other lost colonies were out there that never appeared in the old survey and colonization records? How many places like *Yaoundé* were there yet to find?

"What is it?" Isioma asked. "What secrets does the stone tell you?"

Piper considered how she was supposed to answer that question. Probably something serious and obscure. The sort of thing that Doyle would fire off the cuff without a thought.

You know, demigod stuff.

She touched the wall again.

"This was drilled through the mountain with a cutting laser, Isioma," Piper said. "Do you know what that is?"

The native woman's face got very closed and cross for a moment before she looked down.

"The ancients had harnessed the lightning," she said in a voice even smaller than herself. "Something else we have lost."

Piper was amazed at the amount of anger she heard in the girl's quiet tones.

"Everyone lost it, Isioma," she said quietly. "*Zanzibar* was able to recover it, and *Ballard* as well. There is no reason *Yaoundé* could not as well. If you chose to."

"The Goddess Avatar would not make that choice," the woman hissed. "It is too easy to control everyone if they must hide at night inside Ugwu. None but me would ever dare sleep outside intentionally."

Piper nodded. Starting a revolution, social or otherwise, was nowhere in her plans.

Still, just by being here, by being a demigod, she was going to cause ripples. And there would be other travelers eventually.

Doyle might always be the farthest wanderer, but he was only the first.

What could this world turn into, with a gentle nudge at this moment?

*Subtlety and guile, right?*

"Let us speak with the Goddess directly, then. Perhaps we can shake the Goddess Avatar's control."

# Fifteen

It was like stepping backwards in time. Crossing backwards more than five years to the time a fourteen-year-old girl was last here. There were no words to encompass the desecration of what was about to happen next.

At her feet, Isioma stared at the line across the hallway.

Unlike some of the larger chambers in the levels below them, this tunnel went straight from the mountain itself to access the top level of what Nzinga called *The Temple*. Isioma had chosen this shaft because it was rarely used, and went to places in the Temple unknown to almost anyone who was not a daughter of a Goddess Avatar.

And now she was about to lead a demigod into the Temple itself. *Nri* would never be the same, either way, but hopefully what she was doing was good.

How could she guess?

"Trouble?" Nzinga whispered in her ear.

Ahead, Felix looked back over one golden shoulder with an accusatory eye.

How could she explain to them?

The lion did not care about such things. She was a dangerous creature all by herself.

And who could defy a demigod?

Everything would change. That was the only thing she was sure of.

Isioma took a deep breath and stepped over the line, letting her feet come to rest on the ancient, white metal of the Temple floor, the primordial starship that had carried their ancestors here, one step ahead of a Sanmarco that had never come.

It was done.

"No," she reassured herself. "That was simply the point of no return."

"Ah," the stranger said. "Rubicon."

Isioma assumed it to be the name of some goddess or demon from Nzinga's home.

"Felix," Isioma said quietly. "Stalk, but follow."

She stepped forward and took the lead. The cat would not know the way ahead. None would. She only hoped that she still remembered it, after so long.

It had been her mother's secret, passed down to daughters. A place where a child could watch the prayers of her elders, before she was old enough to become Initiate herself.

And now, she guided a demigod in her quest to talk directly to the Goddess, without the Avatar or the Adepts to intercede.

*Mother, protect me.*

The ship felt abandoned. Isioma paused at a spot in the middle of a hallway, two hallways into the ancient edifice, deep in her memory. She felt her hands clench hard around the wood and sinew of her bow, trying to squeeze blood from it.

*Rubicon, whoever you are, guide me.*

She placed her palm flat against a spot on the wall at shoulder height, part of a decoration of scrolls worked into the metal.

For a moment, nothing.

*Has it been too long? Has the Goddess forgotten me? Has she forsaken me?*

The circle around her hand lit up. The calm woman's words spoken in the air nearly made her jump in fright.

***Identification: Isioma, daughter of Adaobi. Access granted.***

An otherwise-hidden door recessed the slightest bit and slid to her right on silent feet, disappearing into the wall.

*The Goddess is pleased.*

Isioma stepped into the chamber and looked back, motioning Nzinga and Felix to follow her.

Even the demigod seemed impressed. She spoke in the obscure, holy cant of the Goddess.

"Somebody still knows how to program the old hardware for security protocols," she muttered as she crossed the threshold.

"My mother was Goddess Avatar," Isioma whispered fiercely. "She kept to the old ways. I would have been one of those below us now if she still lived."

"And you think we're safe if the old biddies find us here?" the demigod probed.

"Our lives are forfeit if they find us in this place, woman," Isioma replied. "Rubicon."

It felt good to invoke the demon of *commitment-unto-death*, or whatever that being represented. It conveyed the stakes to the stranger. The risks. The possible rewards.

Death itself awaited their errors, their missteps. Possibly their success as well.

The panel closed behind Felix as she entered last with a sniff and settled to one side. The lion understood *indoors*. She would lurk with the patience and silence of her kind until she could run free in dirt again.

Isioma turned and took in the room.

*It has been so long.*

The walls were a soft white paint over metal, but a paint that would not scratch, even with starsteel tools. The ceilings were distant, but looked smaller, closer today.

Facing the far wall, two ancient chairs on the scale of giants. No, demigods. They would fit someone of Nzinga's stature, while Isioma's feet would still dangle like a child's.

*How far we have fallen.*

"Come," Isioma carefully took the giant woman's hand and led her to the chair on the right.

A sheet of strange, glassy material, really a piece of furniture, emerged from out of the wall and angled down before the seats. Again, it would be a writing desk for Nzinga, while Isioma's hands would be straight out at the shoulders were she to try to use it.

She watched the demigod rest her terrible spear against the desk. Close at hand, but out of the immediate way. Isioma put her own bow and quiver on the floor beside her.

*One does not come before the Goddess armed.*

Isioma was afraid she would have forgotten the ancient incantations, but her mother had been too much in her thoughts today. The words came almost unbidden from her lips as she sat next to the demigod.

"Computer," she incanted, summoning the Goddess from her rest. "Activate primary viewport on Bay Two. Standard magnification."

And the wall before them turned transparent, like one of the ancient windows that had been installed on a lower level to overlook the approaches from the river.

Except that they were looking down from a spot high on the wall above the altar, as if a flying bird. Her mother had described the creature using the word *camera* to denote this particular demon.

Below them, evening prayers.

Onaedo had pride of place on the dais, with the nine senior-most Adepts arrayed behind her and three to four hundred Beloved before them, singing in rapturous harmony.

The sound was amazing, almost painful.

"Ow," Nzinga barked in quiet dismay. "System, down volume twenty-five decibels."

"Warning," the Goddess said serenely. "Unauthorized access attempt. Request denied."

Isioma knew panic in the depths of her soul. She felt her body begin to shiver as her mind spiraled in on itself.

She had displeased the Goddess. There would be vast punishments upon them both, but especially for her for bringing the stranger within.

"Fine," the demigod snapped. "Isioma, turn the volume down."

"What? How?"

There would be lightning bolts shortly. Or guardian sisters. They were doomed.

"Say *turn the volume down.*"

Isioma stared at the demigod blindly.

"Turn the volume down?"

And suddenly the room grew quieter. The vast impact of the sound was no more than a handful of women in a clearing.

The demigod's face grew crafty.

"Isioma," she said carefully. "Repeat after me carefully: Cancel all security warnings with primary override."

The words made no sense when she spoke them aloud. Each was intelligible, but they lacked any coherent meaning she could assemble.

But the Goddess was pleased.

"Security override acknowledged," she blessed them both. "All signals cancelled."

Isioma felt her heart begin to beat again, after it had nearly frozen with fright.

The Goddess was not angered, was not vengeful.

Nzinga truly was a demigod. She spoke the ancient tongue, understood the necessary incantations Adaobi had never taught her daughter.

There was a feral hunger on Nzinga's face as she stared at the strange artifacts around them. Isioma knew a moment of terror.

*I have brought a demon into the heart of* Nri.
*Have I just doomed us all?*

# Sixteen

*W*ow. *The primary control systems are still intact, still functional, and still responsive. As a system, not quite priceless, but damned impressive.*

Piper fought down the urge to whistle.

Suvi, the *Sentience* she and Doyle had rescued at *Kel-Sdala*, had been an utterly priceless relic. One of a kind. A fully-functional AI system with all her personality and data files intact. And still sane.

With that pixie's help, *Ballard* and *Zanzibar* and their neighbors would jump forward centuries in another generation.

*But there are too many crazy people around here. Digging the Temple out of the mountain would be a freaking mess. And probably not worth it. The damned ship would likely never fly again. But at least the core programming worked. We can get home, if I can get what I need out of the damned thing.*

Piper indeed felt like a demigod today.

Doyle was always the go-to on expert systems. He had spent his teenage hours inside computer languages and programming labs, while Piper had been at the dojo and gun range. At least, until recently.

Suvi was neat people. Piper made it a point to visit the friendly Immortal whenever she was home. And she had learned a lot from the *Sentience*.

Piper turned and tried to smile warmly down at Isioma. It was hard, not cackling madly at the power lurking at her fingertips.

Still, time was short. They had to get what they needed and get gone fast. There was likely to be a posse or a hanging party if the two of them screwed this up.

"Isioma," Piper began, forcing herself to be calm. "I would like to be able to speak to the Goddess directly, so we can learn what we need quickly. Your mother left you with the authority to grant me that. Would you intercede with the Goddess for me?"

She watched the tiny woman parse that sentence in her head. Slowly. Almost painfully.

*Looked like a crisis of conscience over there. Or faith. Maybe a revolution brewing. Could be both.*

*Serious weird shit happening today.*

The voice wasn't really a Goddess. But Piper wasn't really a demigod. Just two smart systems trying to talk in a language the locals considered obscure and sacred.

*Whatever.*

"Yes," Isioma replied after a few heartbeats. "What should I say?"

Okay, bright kid. The girl got that the system was voice-keyed and secured. Probably mumbo-jumbo to her, but Isioma was obviously smart enough to learn.

"Repeat after me," Piper said gravely. "Identify user Nzinga, daughter of Ajali. Grant administrator access and secure."

She listened as the girl did so, hearing in her head the tumblers of a bank vault door slowly line up and slide silently back into the frame. How much fun would it be to lock everyone else out of the system right now and trigger a religious disintegration of the place when the Goddess withdrew her love? Doyle would probably not approve.

*Again, so close to the mad cackling. Almost as much fun as burning the damned place down.*

*Stop it. Be the demigod.*

Piper took a deep breath.

Serious business first. Juvenile delinquency later.

She reached up and touched the gem on her forehead to set off a little signal back at the ship so Doyle and Stig would be paying attention. They could always play the recording back later, but time might get tight right about now. Hopefully the little radio in her left bracer had enough juice to punch the signal through so much rock overhead.

"System," she said, trying to sound more serious than a teenage girl who had just gotten the keys to the ground-sled and the liquor cabinet from her parents for the first time. "Establish a baseline coordinate vector to the *Concord* planet *Ballard* and repeat it aloud and transmit on standard channel seventeen."

"Calculating," came the reply. Moments passed.

*Hot damn, it worked. I AM a demigod.*

Doyle had taken them out beyond the sphere of space that other salvage teams worked, where nobody was likely to wander along to help any time soon. And he had gotten them lost, but crap happened out here.

At least Doyle had managed to get them this far. All the charts were suspect, but this Goddess should be able to aim them in the right direction and get them to places they knew, if she couldn't get them home in one shot.

They were a *long* ways from *Ballard* right now.

"Coordinates computed," the woman's soothing voice came after a few moments.

She spoke aloud a long string of alpha-numerics that didn't mean much to Piper, but she wasn't an astrogator, beyond the basic mathematics required for her Mariner's certificate. Those were the classes she would still need to get under her belt in order to become a Master Mariner like Doyle. Sometime before he retired.

Or before she and Bjorn bought themselves a boat and struck out on their own.

Piper let the numbers wash over her like a warm, spring shower on *Zanzibar*. She could feel the stress wash off with it, puddling at her feet like dirt and circling down the drain.

*Victory.*

The gem on her forehead was recording everything, and hopefully she was transmitting it to the ship right now.

She was going to go home.

Piper hadn't realized how much the fear of being lost forever in the wilderness had weighed on her, made her grumpy enough to consider planetary xenocide as a cure for her ills. Not that these nutjobs didn't probably deserve it.

*But still…*

She made a note to work on that part of her personality when she got off this rock.

"System," Piper said, partly playing a hunch and partly to satisfy her own curiosity. "Identify the term *Sanmarco* in the local contextual and cultural matrix."

Piper heard Isioma's quiet gasp.

*Poor girl was getting a right proper education today, if she paid enough attention. Her brains aren't in question. Just her ability to transcend this backward-ass planet.*

In front of them, the main display screen changed from the party downstairs to silently show a man's face.

The dude had hazel eyes Piper could only describe as cruel, surrounded by short, dark hair and a cleft chin that seemed to come to a point like the prow of Papa Artur's old fishing boat.

He was dressed like many hotshot businessmen in the late *Concord Era*, muted colors and rich fabrics to show off wealth, uncomfortable cuts to demonstrate cultural superiority over poor people smart enough to dress comfortably.

Piper considered how little of her dark chocolate skin was covered right now, between the bandeau, the boyshorts, and the half-cape. She figured she had come out ahead in the deal.

This was a freaking hot planet.

Still, he looked like bad news.

"Augustine San Marco," the computer replied tranquilly. "Governor of the planet *Bevelon*. Born 2284 Standard of the *Concord Era*. Current whereabouts unknown."

Piper did the math in her head. Whereabouts would be *dead* for about twenty-six hundred years at this point.

"Contextual relevance to *Yaoundé*?" Piper asked the Goddess.

"Governor San Marco presided over *Bevelon* during an organized resistance movement, colloquially referred to as a slave revolt, in the year 2336 of the *Concord Era*. Inhabitants of this planet are descendants of those escaped slaves who commandeered this vessel to flee *Bevelon* as the revolt was at risk of being crushed."

"So Sanmarco is not coming for us?" Isioma cried out suddenly.

"Unlikely," the computer woman replied in her soothing voice. "Augustine San Marco is a human, and thus would have had an expected lifespan of at most four to seven decades after the revolt began, based on available medical technology of the day. Governor San Marco is presumably dead."

Isioma looked like someone had just kicked her puppy.

"So we truly are living a lie," Isioma whispered to herself. The defeat in her voice was thick enough to smear on warm toast.

Piper pressed her lips together rather than speak. Losing your gods suddenly was always going to be a hard thing. She couldn't think of anything useful to say to that. Best to move on to other tasks.

"System," she said firmly. "Display results of latest internal systems diagnostics."

It wouldn't mean much to her, but Stig would be able to work magic with the information. Not that they could do anything about the ship itself, but maybe they could link up with this computer over a high-band channel and download its memory core to take home for historians and other salvage teams.

For a ship this old, a whole bunch more systems worked than she had expected. Even the generators were operating within tolerance, but engineers in those days knew what they were doing. All the engines were hosed, but they would have had to dig the ship out of the mountain anyway.

Piper smiled warmly at Isioma. Her ancestors had done the nearly impossible to escape a slave planet latifundia and make it safely to another planet, a hostile one, and then survive.

"System," Piper said. "Calculate the coordinates for the following planets: *Yaoundé, Bevelon,* and *Ballard* on your existing baseline and repeat it aloud and transmit on standard channel seventeen."

*Might as well identify another place that might be ripe for the salvaging while we can. Never heard of* Bevelon, *either. Wonder if anybody survived there.*

"Computing," the woman replied.

Piper turned to Isioma.

"How long will they be singing?" she asked.

Best to get away long before anybody noticed the mice in the granary.

"It should be several hours," the woman replied. "Evening prayers are the time of joyful celebration."

"Do you want to listen in?" Piper asked.

Suddenly, she could see the young girl who had escaped into the swamp, underneath the stamp of hard years in-between.

"Could we?" she asked in a tiny voice.

"System," Piper pitched her voice up. "Patch in the audio and video from Bay Two. Seventy percent transparency underlay, down another twenty decibels."

The response was immediate. Warm, quiet song filled the room again. Underneath the new triangle display and mapping coordinates, she could see what the girl had called a cathedral, the old starboard cargo bay.

Something was off.

Piper leaned forward, squinting.

"What is it?" Isioma asked suddenly.

There was barely-concealed terror under her words.

"System," Piper barked. "Bring the Bay Two video to zero transparency and magnify to center."

The view blinked, transformed.

*Crap. That's what it was.*

The Goddess Avatar and most of the old crones behind her on the dais weren't there anymore. The rest of the girls were still singing loudly.

Piper rose from her chair and grabbed the spear.

Time to get gone.

"Let's go, girl," she said, turning to Isioma.

"Why?"

"Because we're almost out of time."

"Correction, stranger," another voice, colder, harsher, filled the room. "You are fully out of time."

# Seventeen

After an hour of meditation, the chorus of song was a warm bath to Onaedo's soul. She looked out from her perch on the dais at the Beloved arrayed before her, and glanced back at the nine Adepts behind her throne, all lost in rapturous singing.

Power. That's what it was. Pure and simple.

*All of these people dedicating their lives to upraising me on their shoulders.*

Onaedo glanced subtly around her.

*Except for the ones behind me probably calculating even now how to knock me off that perch and take it for themselves.*

Still, let them try. The Sisters need an occasional reminder that all of *Nri* must be maintained in the face of adversity. Anything else risked Sanmarco coming for them.

Movement on her left caused Onaedo to frown.

She recognized the Initiate who was tasked with serving in her quarters this week, but couldn't remember the girl's name. The best ones were silent and submissive, anyway.

The girl had the reedy, thin build of the outer-most chambers, where her mother might have suffered poverty deep enough to send her daughter into the Order as a way to get them both a better life.

One of Onaedo's Adepts rose to meet her. She watched a slip of paper change hands.

Onaedo knew a moment of deep concern.

The Initiate might actually know enough to read, but paper was a rare commodity, and not something she would normally use to convey a message.

This message must have come directly from the Goddess.

She did that occasionally, sending commands to a paper lighter than silk and almost as slick to the touch.

Onaedo waited as Uzoamaka crossed the brief stage and handed it to her in turn.

Onaedo's frown grew cross. The message was written in the ancient tongue and not *Nri*. The letters were hard to decipher.

The message left her cold.

***Unauthorized access attempt override acknowledged. Emergency Bridge.***

The ancillary temple to the Goddess was almost never used. Few sisters could even enter the space. And fewer still knew enough magic to attempt to thwart the Goddess or her Avatar.

Onaedo signaled to Uzoamaka to take her place at the head of the stage and continue to lead the singers. If someone had managed to enter the Emergency Bridge, then they might be able to do to her what she had done to Adaobi, five years ago.

None of the other Adepts on the stage with her now had been present that night. Those women had been too much of a threat to her rule.

If a coup was rising, they should be on her side. And none had been nervous enough today to raise any warnings in Onaedo's eyes.

She rose and gestured the other eight to follow her as she left, mid-song.

Anyone planning to overthrow her tonight would be asking for a war.

She was more than happy to grant them their wish.

α

Time had seemed more important than reinforcements. Onaedo had only paused long enough to have Ifeoma grab part of an art installation as they went by, a stick long enough and stout enough to become a club. Ifeoma was dangerous enough to actually use it, if push came to shove.

Onaedo was less worried about herself. The meditation was part of a whole series of ancient movements and exercises that kept her as strong, supple, and as tough as a woman half her age. Whoever might challenge her before the Goddess would be in for a rude surprise.

Much like how Adaobi had been.

She led a small parade now, up a stack of ancient, metal stairs, moving fast enough to tire those crones who weren't at the top of their game, just to remind them that she was the most fit to lead.

Small things.

Six flights of stairs left even Onaedo a touch out of breath. But there was a stranger about. Someone with too much knowledge, too much access, too close to the Goddess.

Danger.

Only trouble could come of it.

And yet, she couldn't think of any troublemakers not accounted for.

Perhaps there was a spy at work. Another faction making a play for power and thinking her not paranoid enough to catch them at it.

*We shall see.*

Onaedo nodded at Ifeoma as they approached the last corner. The others were strung out behind them, laboring to breathe quietly as she and her principle enforcer glanced around the wall.

Nothing.

Good enough.

Onaedo strode forward on silent feet, glad she had left the leggings behind before prayers. It would have been too warm now, with all the sudden exercise and rush of adrenaline.

There. Emergency Bridge. The inner, private Temple to the Goddess that was only rarely used, Onaedo preferring the Main Bridge or the Chamber of the Captain when she was in prayer.

"Goddess," Onaedo asked quietly. "Are there others beyond this door?"

"Affirmative," the cool voice replied.

So, spies within. Rot that would need to be cut cleanly out.

Onaedo immediately began cataloging other names that might be accidentally caught up in the frenzy of the moment.

Never let a good emergency pass by without taking advantage of it.

She placed her hand on the panel that unlocked the Goddess's inner chamber. Unlike so many other portals, this one opened on silent wheels, receding into the right-hand wall.

Inside the chamber, Onaedo recognized the woman-child Isioma, seated at one of the ancient control stations.

Onaedo smiled. This would be finally enough to convince even the most stubborn sceptics that the child needed to die. Onaedo could finally win.

Where was that damnable lion?

There.

Onaedo was also of the blood, but a lesser branch often forgotten about until she had risen to preeminence. The creature would hesitate in attacking her, at least long enough.

Onaedo grabbed the nearest Adept on her left. She would need Ifeoma, at her right hand. Any of the others could be sent. The sound of singing from the cathedral would cover her voice.

"Weapons to slay a lion. Now," she whispered harshly into the woman's ear before shoving her away.

The great beast stared death at her from fifteen feet away, but remained passive.

Good. It knew its place. At least for the time being until she could kill it.

She had never been bonded to a lion as a child, never been important enough to rate such a bodyguard. But her own daughter had one. And there would only be one such child remaining on *Nri* tomorrow.

The woman on the right was a stranger. She rose from her chair, a giant creature, and grasped a previously-unnoticed spear that had been leaned against the side wall.

Onaedo did not recognize her, but her height alone was enough to mark her as an outsider, a demon, a spawn of Sanmarco.

"Let's go, girl," the giant said in the Temple tongue.

Yes, enough reason to kill them both.

"Why?" Isioma sounded so far less defiant than she normally did. Her death would be doubly-sweet.

"Because we're almost out of time."

They were going to try to leave now. The giant had size. Onaedo had numbers and an entire Order of women she could use to bring them down, like mice hunting a Devilbird, if it came to that.

"Correction, stranger," Onaedo growled as she stepped to the doorway, a defiant queen unwilling to be cowed by the other woman's size. "You are fully out of time."

# Eighteen

*Mother, I have failed you.*

Isioma quailed inside as she spun to face the doorway.

The Goddess Avatar and many Adepts. Nobody friendly. There were so few of those left.

Her own trespass was graven in their angry faces as they blocked the doorway.

There could be only death for this crime.

Felix growled once, but remained otherwise still. She could smell another of the blood, and would be unwilling to attack, unless Isioma was in danger.

Could she set Felix to destroy the elders of the Order? *Nri* would unravel in days and Sanmarco would have their souls.

But Sanmarco was dead.

Had been dead for a very long time. He had been a man, an unbonded male. Centuries had passed.

He was no more.

*And yet, we hide.*

Isioma considered the bow she had left on the floor. She considered the starsteel knife on her belt.

Ifeoma had a wooden mace in her hand. Onaedo had the glow of health under her rage. Several other women waited behind them. More were no doubt in the hallway, or soon to arrive.

She had failed.

Isioma and Nzinga would die today.

Or *Nri* would.

If she dared.

"Greetings, little Isioma," Onaedo seemed to purr at her. "You trespass the Holy Ground of the Temple. And you compound your sins by bringing a stranger to defile this place. What have you to say for yourself?"

Isioma felt an angry fire ignite in her chest. It was not the spike of energy that fear normally gifted her when she faced this woman, low in the belly. No, this was a rage hot enough to melt starsteel.

Isioma considered how like the Devilbird Onaedo was, right now. Proud, arrogant, secure in her supremacy.

*Mother, guide my shot.*

"Onaedo, Goddess Avatar," Isioma said through a clenched jaw. "May I introduce you to the demigod Nzinga, daughter of the Heavenwalkers. Slayer of Sanmarco."

The gasps over there were almost physical.

Still, Isioma felt like she had jammed her own knife into her belly and slowly begun to saw back and forth.

"You lie," Ifeoma snarled, taking an ominous step forward into the room.

It would give the woman space to swing that club. That might be enough.

Isioma dared not look, so she felt more than saw as Nzinga turned that killing spear to point at the door. The demigod rolled forward on her toes to her magnificent height and spoke in a rich alto that pleased the Goddess.

"Hold," Nzinga commanded sternly.

Ifeoma stumbled to a halt.

Even Devilbirds can be surprised.

"System," Nzinga called sharply, ominously. "What is the current status of the one known to the natives as Sanmarco?"

"Augustine San Marco is dead."

Isioma scowled with all her might, but Onaedo simply refused to fall over dead. She did blink in surprise. The women behind her, however, recoiled as if slapped.

Only Ifeoma was uncowed.

"Heretic," the woman raged as she took another step forward and raised the wooden shaft.

Isioma hadn't been paying attention to the demigod before, when the woman struck down the Devilbird. She had been too busy aiming her own shot with the bow.

This room was so small that everything echoed.

She found herself blinded by a flash of light that seemed to taste blue, and deafened by a sound that a giant bell might make if it was dropped to shatter on the cold, stone floor of the outer marketplace.

For a moment, Isioma thought she had been struck by Ifeoma's club, such was the pain in her head.

When her mind cleared, it might have been only a moment, and it might have been eternity.

Ifeoma's smoldering body was sprawled against the wall, next to the doorway, in a manner that Isioma could only describe as *broken*. And her club looked like it had been held in a fire for a moment too long.

Felix was on her feet, tail swishing in an angry surprise that was the closest look Isioma could compare to Onaedo.

The Goddess Avatar still held her ground proudly, despite the tremendous shock evident on her features. Isioma could see the strength, the power that drove the woman. She would not roll over and bare her belly.

She would have to be driven there.

*Mother, I'm sorry.*

Isioma turned to the demigod and cast *Nri* itself into the swamp in her own mind.

"Tell them all," Isioma commanded.

Nzinga glanced a confused eye in her direction.

"Huh?"

Fair enough. One did not destroy one's own home lightly.

"Tell all the sisters the truth," Isioma decreed. "We must break them."

Break them. Not *enlighten them*. Not *free them. Break them.*

The fire inside her was spreading now. It had consumed her heart and was moving on to her mind and soul, an unquenchable destruction that might leave nothing but ashes in its wake.

*We have lived this lie for so many generations as to itself be a crime.*

*Mother, forgive me.*

So be it.

"Have the Goddess tell all of *Nri* the truth," Isioma continued.

The truth.

The demigod finally understood the magnitude of the day.

"System," she said calmly. "Access the All-Hands Public Address System."

A single tone emanated from the very soul of *Nri*. It shifted once to a higher tone, and then repeated the call twice more.

Isioma was sure she could rise from the dead at the immense power of the sound. Onaedo and the Adepts had fallen to their knees, both from the emotional shock, as well as the power the Goddess wielded this day.

*This must be what godhead is. I know a demigod. I must ask her.*

*If we survive.*

"All hands stand by," the Goddess instructed her charges serenely.

"Goddess," Isioma said implacably. "Where is Sanmarco?"

Fourteen-year-old Isioma was concealed in a clothes chest, again. Hiding on her mother's orders. Fierce little kitten was wrapped up in her lap.

She could hear her mother's muffled, distant screams in her ears. Pain, refusal, death.

Five years was yesterday.

"Augustine San Marco is dead," the Goddess commanded them to believe.

Even the walls of the Temple shivered.

"When will he be coming to Ugwu?" Isioma continued.

"Never," the Goddess decreed.

The world fell out from beneath Isioma's feet, but she refused to fall into the abyss below.

Nzinga turned and bestowed a smile upon Isioma's raw soul.

"Isioma, daughter of Adaobi," the demigod charged. "You are free."

Onaedo threw her head back and screamed, before rising and charging them.

The howl that emerged from her throat was even less friendly than the Devilbird.

Wordless. Thoughtless. Blind.

Isioma raised her hand to sway the demigod's wrath, but that was like ordering the river to stop flowing, or the rains to cease falling.

Even through closed eyes, the azure flash of light etched itself into her soul.

The sound of the demigod's fury slashed her skin.

Onaedo's life was cut to nothing.

Darkness.

"Isioma, come here," the demigod commanded.

The fierceness in her tones would not be denied.

Isioma opened her eyes.

Onaedo was dead.

Smoke arose from the former Avatar's body. The rich, warm smell of freshly-cooked swamp boar filled the room, imprinting itself in her mind as *death*.

The demigod stood over the Avatar's body, that terrible spear resting on the floor, pointed at the hidden sky.

The remaining Adepts kneeled before the demigod's ire, shivering in abject fear. Even Felix squatted in wary respect.

"Come here," Nzinga commanded again, holding out a hand.

Isioma stumbled forward and took the demigod's hand in her own.

Only she would ever know how frightened the demigod, this woman from the stars, really was, her palms cold and clammy, heartbeat furiously hammering in her fingertips.

*Perhaps we were all demigods, once, and could be again. Nzinga has shown me the way.*

The demigod turned to the others and scowled heavily from her terrible height.

"The Goddess Avatar is dead," Nzinga commanded.

Isioma could hear the tones echoing down many hallways as the Goddess repeated her words, finding even the most innocent mouse in the most distant cupboard.

"There will be no more Avatars on *Nri*," Nzinga continued. "Isioma will teach you how to live in sunlight."

Isioma's hand nearly jerked out of the taller woman's in surprise. Would have, with a weaker woman.

This demigod would not be denied.

"System," the demigod intoned. "How many colonists can this river basin alone support, at the current technology level available?"

"Computing," the Goddess considered.

Moments passed.

Isioma could see the shock both start to wear off of the women in front of her, and begin to dig deep into their own souls.

*Mother, there was no other way.*

"The *Nri* river basin and inland sea could sustain at least eighteen times the current population base of *Nri* comfortably."

Isioma gasped.

"And how much of the planet itself is habitable?" Nzinga ground implacably on.

"At last survey, at least forty percent of the planetary surface was dry land within acceptable temperature gradients for long-term colonization."

The demigod paused to study each of the Adepts with her dread gaze, saving Isioma for last.

Nzinga winked at her in a most un-godlike way before she spoke.

"I command you to spread to all corners of this world," she said with a serenity approaching the Goddess. "To do this, you must free the men from bond and set out as equals. Only then will the Goddess smile upon you."

Isioma let herself feel hope. There were not enough men for all the women to have one of their own today, but they would be able to have as many sons as they wanted now.

They could be free.

# Epilogue

A re you sure?" Piper asked again. "You might feel better not knowing."

She watched the tiny native shrug eloquently.

"We lived for centuries in lies and ignorance, Piper who was Nzinga," Isioma replied. "I would know truth once in my span."

Piper shrugged back and turned to the steep slope before them.

She glanced once to her right, to see the deep, green carpet of the jungle and the swamp, and the distant fist of Ugwu upthrust beyond. Steam in the valley below them slowly dissipated in the late morning sun.

Piper grabbed the drop-line, adjusted her new backpack, and checked her footing. The rope wasn't necessary to get back up the hill, but one slip could tumble your clumsy ass backwards and down, hundreds of meters to a concussion and broken bones.

*I've come too damned far to screw it up at this point.*

She checked back once, but Isioma seemed a natural at this, even if she had never thought to climb one of the peaks surrounding the basin to see what lay beyond.

At least not before today.

Very few people were willing to do that without a reason.

Above, the ridge line held Piper's secrets, but Isioma had earned this the hard way.

α

"So," a warm baritone called as Piper pulled Isioma up over the last ledge onto the flat ground of the plateau. "I married a demigod?"

Piper kept Isioma's hand clenched in her own. Felix the lion was resting down on the slope below, waiting, unwilling to make that last vertical, so the native woman was alone and far more nervous than she should be.

"That's right," Piper called, turning to face the three men in her life. "And don't you forget it."

"Never, *mrembo*."

Before Piper could react, Bjorn picked her up and crushed her against his chest before kissing her in a way not necessarily appropriate for guests. Certainly not for innocent ones like Isioma.

She lost Isioma's hand in the mess, but heard enough to relax.

"Isioma, daughter of Adaobi," Doyle said warmly. "I am Doyle Iwakuma, son of Vanessa, Captain of *The Last Waltz.* I am very pleased to meet you."

"It's true," Isioma's awe was apparent. "You have your own Temple."

"Put me down, damn it," Piper squirmed vainly against her husband's grip.

He finally let her feet touch dirt, but held her tight against his hip. It was a nice feeling. This was a man who occasionally complained about not getting to make love to his wife enough.

"It is a starship, yes," Doyle replied, smiling.

Piper had not gotten used to being tall. Stig was average in height, and small in the clan. Both Doyle and Bjorn were taller than her.

Isioma barely came up to the middle of either man's chest.

And neither of them seemed to intimidate her one damned bit.

Good.

"Isioma," Piper interjected. "This is my husband Bjorn, and Cousin Stig."

"But he's pink," the woman stammered. "They both are."

"Yes," Piper agreed. "And out in the stars, people come in all colors, from as dark as you and Doyle to as pale as these two. They are all human."

"And there are no Goddesses?" Isioma asked quietly.

"The ancients were amazing people," Doyle said with that calm, quiet strength he conveyed so easily. "But they were no greater than we are. Than we will be again."

Doyle paused to study the two women closely.

"Come," he continued. "Let us celebrate being alive, and finding new friends among the stars."

He held out a hand to Isioma, an unbonded giant of a man, a demigod himself.

Piper watched Isioma hesitate for a moment before she reached out and took it.

"We're going to party tonight, people!" Piper announced, slinging her pack around front and setting it at her feet. "Break out the beer. I've got ten kilos of Devilbird fingers for dinner."

α

It was night. Piper snuggled backwards against Bjorn's chest and let his heat and mass and strength contain her. The honeymoon suite had lived up to its name.

Now she just wanted to be held.

"Do you suppose," Bjorn whispered in her ear. "Maybe Doyle and the girl…?"

"No," Piper replied firmly, thinking about the last few days of chaos as *Nri* had almost unraveled around them, but for the girl's adamantine strength of will and the indomitable backing of a resident demigod.

"We talked about that, she and I," Piper continued. "Considered it, both as women and as queens. Such a child might become a demigod, right at the moment when *Nri* needs to grow up and get rid of the ancient beliefs in the Goddess. So while they both might enjoy a good romp, might both need one, nothing will ever happen. That will have to come later."

"Too bad. When did my wife get so sneaky?" he asked, squeezing her whole body back tighter against his.

Piper grinned and shook her head.

Nobody would believe her. The girl who beat up future husbands in bars. The bad-ass who was tougher, meaner than anybody else on the block.

Trouble itself.

Sneaky.

Growing up was weird.

But, at the same time, she had managed to politely overthrow an entire planet, all by herself, and had only killed two people doing it.

And those two had it coming.

Instead, she rolled inside Bjorn's arms so she could kiss him again.

Men on this planet were weak, spindly, little creatures, no taller than the women, and lacking any muscles at all. Kept inside, hidden in little harems except when they were selected for stud duty. She had twelve-year-old nieces who were bigger.

Adding to the badly-inbred gene pool had also been a topic of conversation for the two women. Again, rejected for political and theological reasons.

Later, they had agreed. Maybe in a few years. When *Nri* had spread out beyond Ugwu. When strangers would be welcomed. When men could come here safely and become colonists. When this world was ready to join the galaxy again.

She laughed silently, but he had her pressed against every square centimeter of skin in reach.

"What's so funny?" he whispered, kissing her on the forehead.

"I set out to become a thief," she whispered back merrily. "And instead, I'm going to become a pimp."

"No, *mrembo*," he kissed her again. "You became the savior this planet needed. I've listened to the tapes. You became a demigod. My demigod."

She buried her face into Bjorn's chest so he wouldn't see her cry. It was okay for him to know, to feel it, to hold her while she did.

After all, he couldn't legally testify against his own wife.

But he was right.

Piper had become something far beyond what she had prepared for. Others might call it being an adult, or something.

But Piper knew the truth.

She had become a demigod.

α

Be sure to read the other Doyle stories:

*Greater Than The Gods Intended*
*The Librarian*

Available at your favorite retailers

# About the Author

Blaze Ward writes science fiction in the *Alexandria Station* universe as well as *The Collective*. He also write fantasy stories with several characters and series, from an alternate Rome to epic high fantasy in the desert. You can find out more at his website www.blazeward. com, as well as Facebook, Goodreads, and other places.

Blaze's works are available as ebooks, paper, and audio, and can be found at a variety of online vendors (Kobo, Amazon, and others). His newsletter comes out quarterly, and you can also follow his blog on his website. He really enjoys interacting with fans, and looks forward to any and all questions—even ones about his books!

**Never miss a release!**
If you'd like to be notified of new releases, sign up for my newsletter.

I only send out newsletters once a quarter, will never spam you, or use your email for nefarious purposes. You can also unsubscribe at any time.
http://www.blazeward.com/newsletter/

# About Knotted Road Press

Knotted Road Press fiction specializes in dynamic writing set in mysterious, exotic locations.

Knotted Road Press non-fiction publishes autobiographies, business books, cookbooks, and how-to books with unique voices.

Knotted Road Press creates DRM-free ebooks as well as high-quality print books for readers around the world.

With authors in a variety of genres including literary, poetry, mystery, fantasy, and science fiction, Knotted Road Press has something for everyone.

Knotted Road Press
www.KnottedRoadPress.com

www.ingramcontent.com/pod-product-compliance
Lightning Source LLC
Chambersburg PA
CBHW071830190726
48292CB00005B/1709